"Now you're older.

Natalie continued to stare at him, arms crossed, the toe of her purple clog tapping on the floor.

"And smarter."

"I don't want anything to happen to Austin," she said after a moment. "He's all I've got."

She didn't meet his gaze as she said the words, but he could see how much they cost her. He felt a rush of emotion and a spark of envy. It was irrational and unfair, but Liam didn't have anything—anyone—so precious to him in his life. He hadn't since he'd left Crimson.

"I'll keep him safe, Natalie." He couldn't stop himself from touching her, just a finger on the delicate bone at her wrist. "I'll keep both of you safe."

She went still as his finger grazed her skin. "I'm overreacting," she said after a moment, shifting away from his touch. "It will be fun. Thank you for including us." The words were as stiff as her body language, but Liam didn't press her on it. He wasn't sure what, if anything, he wanted from Natalie again—but he had an entire holiday season to figure it out.

* * *

A VERY CRIMSON CHRISTMAS

BY
MICHELLE MAJOR

MILLS &
BOON

Published in Great Britain 2015
by Mills & Boon, an imprint of Harlequin (UK) Limited,
Eton House, 18-24 Paradise Road, Richmond, Surrey, TW9 1SR

© 2015 Michelle Major

ISBN-13: 978-0-263-25184-5

23-1115

Harlequin (UK) Limited's policy is to use papers that are natural, renewable and recyclable products and made from wood grown in sustainable forests. The logging and manufacturing processes conform to the legal environmental regulations of the country of origin.

Printed and bound in Spain
by CPI, Barcelona

Michelle Major grew up in Ohio but dreamed of living in the mountains. Soon after graduating with a degree in journalism, she pointed her car west and settled in Colorado. Her life and house are filled with one great husband, two beautiful kids, a few furry pets and several well-behaved reptiles. She's grateful to have found her passion writing stories with happy endings. Michelle loves to hear from her readers at www.michellemajor.com.

To Wendy. Thanks for being a fabulous friend
and for loving the Indian buffet as much as I do.

Chapter One

Natalie Holt blinked open one eye and slapped her hand against the alarm clock blaring out heavy metal music. Heavy metal wasn't typically popular in the mountains, but she'd managed to tune in to a college station situated a few towns over from where she lived in Crimson, Colorado.

Not her preference, but she slept through every other genre from classical to country to talk radio. Even the annoying default alarm buzz couldn't jolt her awake these days. Probably a result of averaging about four hours of sleep each night.

Last night had been closer to three hours since she'd stayed up to finish the month-end medical billing for the senior living center where she worked. She'd been lucky to pick up the extra position—her official third job. She needed the money but couldn't afford to take any more time away from her nine-year-old son, Austin. A decent night's sleep was one of the few expendable items on her schedule.

Austin was the best thing in her life, and Natalie would manage through bleary-eyed sleep deprivation or walk on hot coals if it meant keeping him safe. Even if she collapsed from utter exhaustion in the process.

But she wasn't dead yet, so she dragged herself out of bed and threw on a sweatshirt and pair of black yoga pants that hadn't seen the inside of a yoga studio for years. It was Saturday morning, which she hoped meant Austin was still asleep. When she found the door to his room open she expected to find him at the computer or in front of the TV. Instead, the farmhouse where they'd been living for the past several months was quiet.

She headed down the stairs toward the hallway that led to the master bedroom, but something caught her eye out the front window. Shading her eyes against the bright morning light, she stepped onto the porch, wrapping her arms around herself to ward off the frigid temperatures. It was the start of December, so the cold air and dusting of snow on the flagstone porch were to be expected, but still a shock. Not smart to brave the cold precoffee.

An enormous black SUV sat in the driveway, and a shiver of unease slithered up her spine. Who would be paying such an early morning visit to Ruth Keller, the elderly woman who owned the property? And where was her son at this hour of the day?

She turned and went back into the house. The farmhouse had been remodeled with two distinct sections, the bedrooms on one side and the main living area with the kitchen, dining room, office and family room on the other. Her heart raced, then slowed as she found Austin curled on Ruth's bed with her, reading aloud from one of his beloved *Magic Tree House* series of books.

"Hey, Mom, I'm keeping Miss Ruth company." He smiled, showing off the gap between his two front teeth. Orthodontia was definitely a part of their future, but Natalie would put off that financial worry for another day.

Ruth's smile was softer. "Good morning, dearie. I hope you weren't worried about Austin."

"Not at all," Natalie lied. "But next time wake me up before you come downstairs. Okay, bud?"

"Sure, Mom."

"And maybe you should give Miss Ruth some room on the bed. I don't want you to put any pressure on her hip."

Ruth placed a hand on Austin's arm when he went to move. "He's fine. I like the company."

Natalie didn't doubt that for a second. Ruth Keller was a firecracker of a woman, even pushing her mideighties. She liked to be independent and active, which was why she'd initially hired Natalie to help with her care. According to Ruth, Natalie was the only nurse in town who didn't treat her as if she had one foot in the grave. Natalie had been happy to coordinate doctors' appointments, buy groceries and help around the house in exchange for using the two upper guest bedrooms. But Ruth had insisted on paying her as well, and Natalie was in no position to refuse the money. A few weeks ago, Ruth had fallen and bruised her hip, which increased Natalie's responsibilities.

She knew Ruth was terrified of eventually ending up in assisted living, despite the fact that she already had a room paid for each month at the senior center. Natalie had vowed to help out as much as she could to make sure that Ruth could stay at the farmhouse as long as possible. There was another home-care nurse who came in for respite shifts, but it was a lot for Natalie to balance with her schedule at the senior center and the medical billing work. Natalie was determined to handle everything.

She'd learned a long time ago that the only person she could depend on in life was herself.

"How about breakfast?"

"The man's making it," Austin informed her, then went back to reading.

"Don't get too far ahead." Ruth tapped the page with one bony finger.

"The man?" Natalie took a step closer to the bed, remembering the luxury SUV parked in front of the house. Her skin suddenly tingled. "What man?"

"I must have forgotten to mention it to you." Ruth straightened the covers over her lap, keeping her eyes averted. "Austin, what happens next? Do Jack and Annie find the ninja?"

"Mention what?" Natalie asked, reaching forward to grip the bedpost. "Who's here, Ruth?"

"Hello, Natalie," a long-forgotten voice said from the doorway behind her.

Her fingers tightened around the wood until her knuckles went white.

"You remember Liam Donovan," Ruth said cheerfully, although she still wouldn't meet Natalie's gaze. "The two of you knew each other in high school."

Breathing was supposed to be an involuntary muscle reflex, but in that moment Natalie forgot how to draw air into her lungs. Concentrating, she forced her breath in and out. Saying she'd known Liam Donovan was like claiming Elizabeth Taylor and Richard Burton once had a passing acquaintance.

She turned, keeping her features a placid mask as stormy gray eyes clashed with hers. "It's been a long time, Liam. Nice to see you." Which was partly the truth. Yes, it had been over ten years since she'd spoken to Liam Donovan. But *nice* didn't begin to describe how it felt to be in the same room as him after all this time. It made her feel nauseous, invigorated, desperately sad and filled with regret. But not nice. Her feelings for Liam had never been nice.

One side of his mouth lifted as if he found her outright lie amusing. The smile didn't reach his eyes, and the storm inside them cooled by several degrees. "I'm here to visit Ruth, to make sure she's okay after her fall. And to find out why I'm paying for housing every month at assisted living when she's still here even though she's been injured." Ruth had been Liam's nanny when he was younger, but Natalie knew the woman loved him as if he was her own family.

"She fell two weeks ago and is almost fully recovered." Natalie didn't try to stop the censure in her voice. "She's worked out how she wants to handle her room at the center with the director, so you'll need to discuss that with him. I can assure you she's well cared for. I've got it under control."

His gaze flicked to Austin, whose nose was once again buried in the book. "So I see."

She wondered for a moment what exactly Liam thought he saw. The boy who had been her first love was gone, replaced by a man who was so much larger, both in physical build and general presence. Liam had been beautiful in high school but now there was a raw masculinity to his features. He'd filled into his height and the potential of his looks. His hair was shorter than he'd worn it back then, the cut clearly from an expensive salon. It had darkened to almost black but remained streaked with the same chestnut shine she'd always loved to run her fingers through.

Even now her fingers itched to reach out and touch him, to prove that he was here before her, not just a visitor to her unwanted dreams and fantasies, as he'd been so many times in the past decade.

She ran a self-conscious hand through her own hair, several weeks past due for a trim and years from her last professional highlight. Her shoulders inched a little straighter. Pride was one of the few things so many years of struggling hadn't taken from Natalie. As the only weapon left in her arsenal, she would use it without apology.

Before she could reply, Austin scooted off the bed to stand next to her. "My mom is Miss Ruth's nurse," he said, his small chin jutting forward. "She's really good at it. Miss Ruth needs us."

For better or worse, Austin had inherited both her pride and her stubborn nature. He was unfailingly protective of her and didn't even blink under Liam's scrutiny. She imagined grown men in boardrooms cowering before that stare, but not her beautiful boy. She gave him a small squeeze.

"I'm sure Ruth is happy to have you here, Liam."

He gave the barest hint of a nod as he continued to study her son.

"Austin, sweetie, why don't you finish the story with Miss Ruth while Liam helps me with breakfast?"

"That's a great idea," Ruth piped in behind them. "Happy reunions always make me hungry."

Natalie threw Ruth a look over her shoulder and the older woman winked.

"I can help, Mom. I'm good at making coffee."

"That you are, big guy." She bent down to kiss his cheek, then whispered in his ear, "Miss Ruth needs you more this morning. Liam and I can handle breakfast. We're fine."

Clearly reluctant, Austin narrowed his eyes at Liam before turning to climb back on the bed.

Liam held out his arm, indicating that Natalie should lead him to the kitchen. She tried to hold her breath as she walked by him, but his scent twined through her senses as if by osmosis. He'd changed something in the years since she'd known him, his soap or shampoo maybe. But underneath remained a trace of something that was all Liam, clean and a little spicy. Unfortunately, parts of her that didn't involve her brain had an immediate reaction to him. She reached out for the wall to steady herself.

"Cute kid," Liam mumbled as she passed him.

Her temper quickly roared to life. "He's an *amazing* kid. We're a team."

"What about Brad?" he asked as he followed her through the house.

She cringed at the mention of her ex-husband. "He's not part of Austin's life. He left Crimson and never looked back." Not exactly the whole truth, but as much as she was willing to share with Liam Donovan. For good measure she added, "I seem to have that effect on men."

When she glanced back Liam was frowning.

"You have no idea the effect you have on men, Natalie. You never did."

Oh. *Well.* She didn't know how to take that.

She moved to the refrigerator as a distraction and took out a carton of eggs, cheese and juice. "What are you doing back in Crimson? Ruth's hip is healing just fine. In another week or so, she should be cleared to drive again. I don't believe you're here to see to her welfare."

"She practically raised me until I was eleven. I love that woman."

She rolled her eyes as she put a pan on the stove, then began to crack eggs into a small mixing bowl. "I know.

And she thinks the sun rises and sets by you. It doesn't answer the question."

"I'm here to see to her welfare." As he stepped closer to her, Natalie worked to keep her fingers from trembling. He handed her an egg and she took it, making sure not to touch him in the process.

She could feel him watching her but kept her attention focused on the task in front of her.

"I believe someone is stealing money from my former nanny," Liam said after a moment. Her gaze crashed into his as he continued, "I'm wondering if it might be you."

Liam wasn't sure how he wanted Natalie to react to his little bombshell. He'd said it more for the shock value because he wanted her as off balance as he felt. A part of him expected her to throw a fit or crack an egg over his head as she screamed out her denial. Instead, she placed the egg on the counter as she went brittlely still.

"Is that really what you think of me?" she asked, her gaze flaring as she watched him.

No, never, a voice inside him wanted to argue. *I think you are still the most beautiful woman I've ever seen.*

Even the ratty sweatshirt she wore couldn't cover Nat's perfect figure. Her dark hair pulled back in a messy ponytail was still shiny and looked as soft as he remembered from years ago. She wore no makeup, but he'd always preferred her that way. Unlike when they were in high school, she now had faint circles under those big melted chocolate eyes that told him something was keeping her awake at night. Liam found himself wanting to know what it was and figure out a way to fix her troubles.

But that wasn't what this trip was about. Natalie had made her choice years ago. She'd picked this town over him. He wasn't about to come crawling back to her.

"I don't know what to think, Nat. You came to work for her and two months later almost ten thousand dollars is missing from her account."

"Did you ask her about it?"

"Of course I did. I called her when the accountant alerted me. She told me to mind my own business."

"Which wasn't an option for you?"

"She's a strong woman, but not as strong as she once was, either mentally or physically. You're her nurse so you must see that she's frail. I won't let someone take advantage of her."

"I would never do that."

"But you haven't denied taking the money and you've let her return to the house when I arranged for assisted living."

She looked up at him now, her brown eyes blazing. "I didn't steal anything, Liam."

Her voice was quiet but lethal. Liam realized he'd misread her stillness. He thought it might be masking guilt, but now he saw she was reining in her anger. Anger that he would accuse her of something so awful.

"I'm sorry, Natalie. The way the accountant spoke it was too much of a coincidence to ignore. You started working for her and soon after money goes missing from her savings account."

"Does she know you're monitoring her finances?"

Liam blew out a breath. "She does now." He watched as she put two bagels in the toaster, then poured the egg mixture into the heated pan. "She's mad as all get out."

"Do you blame her?"

"I want to keep her safe. People know I've settled money on her and that she barely touches it. I would have expected someone to take advantage of her long before this. That's why I keep track of things."

"All signs to the contrary in your life, you can't always bully or manipulate people into doing what you want. Ruth can make her own decisions about her savings."

"Trust me, I know very well that not everyone bends to my will just because I want them to." He thought of a night long ago when Natalie had made him believe his heart was breaking in half. "But why is she acting like she doesn't know what I'm talking about? Why isn't she the least bit concerned the money is gone? That's not like her. She's hiding something. Maybe it's not that someone is stealing from her. But there's more to what's going on. I'm going to find out what it is."

He saw her fingers tighten around the handle of the pan. "Either way, I'm sure Ruth will be glad to see you. If you want to use the guest bedrooms upstairs, Austin and I can move out."

"Natalie." He placed his fingers on her shoulder. His chest took a direct hit as she flinched at the contact. "Kicking you out or waging some kind of war with you was never my intention."

She took a stack of plates from the cupboard, her sweatshirt rising above the waistband of her pants as she reached for a high shelf. His mind went blank for a moment at the sight of the creamy strip of skin across her lower back and the small birthmark that peeked out from her hip. Memories flooded back to him, along with a rush of heat to the lower half of his body.

"You accused me of stealing from a woman we both love. How is that not waging war?"

He shook his head to bring himself back to the present. "I had to be sure."

"And you are now?" Something about her tone and the way she wouldn't make eye contact with him made his skin prickle with doubt.

"I'm not getting the whole story, but I will figure it out."

"Go for it," she snapped back quickly. "I don't have Ruth's money."

Her movements jerky, she dished eggs, bagels and sliced bananas onto the plates.

"It wouldn't matter if you did," an unsteady voice called. "Thanks to Liam, I have plenty to spare."

Liam turned as Ruth and Austin appeared in the doorway to the kitchen. His breath caught as he watched her lean heavily on a carved wooden cane. He'd arrived in Crimson late last night, so he hadn't seen his former nanny before this morning. Knowing she was an early riser like him, he'd come to the property at the crack of dawn. She'd been awake but still in bed, so he hadn't fully noticed how frail she looked compared to the hearty, healthy woman he once knew. Ruth had always been larger than life, the only constant he'd known for most of his childhood. She'd seen his shock this morning and had immediately sent him off to survey her property.

After checking to make sure things looked good around the house and small pond near the edge of the forest, he'd returned to the house to find Austin curled up next to her in her bed. Liam had never been the type of kid to snuggle with anyone, let alone his nanny. He'd been too busy getting into trouble as a kid. He envied Natalie's son the easy affection he had with both his mom and Ruth. Austin was clearly loved, a thought that gave Liam an unfamiliar stab of envy for what he'd only felt as a boy from the paid help.

"That isn't the point."

"Leave her alone." Ruth straightened and pointed at him. "Sit down and have breakfast with us. Stop harping on Natalie. I'm glad to see you. Don't make me change my mind."

"There isn't—" he began at the same time Natalie handed him a plate. "You made enough for me?"

"When I cook it's for whoever is here to eat." She picked up the three remaining plates, balancing two in one hand. With her opposite elbow she pointed to a drawer at the end of the kitchen island. "Bring forks over with you."

He stared at her.

"Please," she added as an afterthought.

"I don't eat breakfast."

"It's the most important meal of the day."

Ruth lowered herself into a chair and patted the one next to her. "Come on over. Catch me up on your life." She leaned closer to Austin. "Liam is powerful. He has lots of money and dates gobs of brainless supermodels who are too young for him."

"Ruth, stop."

"Are you a supermodel, Mom?" Austin asked.

Natalie set down the plates with a clatter. "No, bud, I'm not a supermodel."

Her son nodded, looking relieved.

Natalie brushed by Liam to get the orange juice and glasses, her mouth tight with obvious disapproval.

He wanted to tell her she was more enticing than any model he'd ever known. She was a real woman, and it was more than her physical beauty that had made Natalie irresistible. It was the way she carried herself, how she knew who she was, the fact that she wouldn't ever take any crap from him.

He slid into the seat next to Ruth instead. "You can't stay here," he said, changing the subject back to the argument they'd been having before she sent him off to look over the property this morning.

"It's my home."

"It's too much for you. You'll move in with me while

I'm here and we get the property ready to go on the market. When I leave, you'll go to assisted living. Why am I paying for a room there if you don't use it?"

"Because I like the social activities. They only let residents go on outings. You have the money, so I didn't think you'd mind." Ruth forked up a slice of banana, the tremor in her hand clearly visible.

"Are you selling the farmhouse?" Natalie looked shocked.

"No," Ruth answered at the same time Liam said, "Yes."

"Ten acres is too much for her, too far away from town—"

"That's why Natalie and Austin are here. And I have Clarence come by for a few hours every day to maintain things."

"Clarence is almost as old as you."

"Don't sass me, Liam." Ruth stabbed at her eggs with the fork. "I'll have Stan give you extra chores when he gets home from work."

Liam glanced at Natalie, who gave a sharp shake of her head. Ruth's husband, Stan, had died the same year she retired and they moved to Colorado. He wasn't sure if he should argue with her or let the comment pass. After a moment he sighed, trying to remember that he had to tread lightly with his former nanny. She'd always been fiercely independent. Liam had gotten used to people doing what he said without question. In the space of an hour, these two women and one boy had given him more trouble than he'd had in years.

"I just want to take care of you."

"If you're only here to pester me, you might as well leave now."

He knew she meant it. Her heart was as big as the Rocky Mountains, but Ruth Keller didn't mince words.

"Is it so hard to believe I missed you?"

"It's hard to believe you haven't been to see me in two years," Ruth answered, her gaze shrewd.

She could believe her husband who'd been dead for over fifteen years was coming home yet still intuit that Liam was hiding something from her. Liam had to respect the way her mind still worked. He also had to come up with another reason to stay in town so he could get to the bottom of what was happening with her money. "I'm working on my own software company—it's a new type of GPS technology for outdoor activities. It's called LifeMap. Besides wanting to see you, I'm looking at basing the company in Crimson. I know how much you love this town and I thought it would make you happy if I could give a boost to the local economy."

She studied him for a moment, then reached out and wrapped her veined hand around his. "I like the sound of that. You're a good boy, Liam. Much better than either of your parents. I raised your father, just like I raised you. And I certainly raised him to do better than that gold-digging mother of yours. She always resented me because I knew how to take care of you better than she did. No offense, sweetie."

"None taken," Liam said with a smile. "When was the last time you talked to Mom?"

"She sends flowers on my birthday," Ruth said without hesitation. "Pink roses."

"You hate roses." He looked up as Natalie clapped a hand over her mouth.

"I know," Ruth answered. "Liam's mother does, too. She sends them anyway."

Liam closed his eyes for a moment, anger building at his parents for all the things they didn't care about because they were too busy with their own lives. When he opened them again, Natalie was watching him with a look in her eyes that he didn't want to believe was pity.

"What do you think?" he asked her, his voice tight. He could take her anger and irritation, but pity he had to shut down immediately. "Should she stay in this house alone when I'm paying for a room at Evergreen?"

"She's not alone," Austin offered around a mouthful of food. "She's got us."

Liam raised an eyebrow at Natalie. "Not the point."

"It's up to Ruth to decide where she wants to live, but I think you've been generous."

"You won't mind if she sells this place and moves to Evergreen full-time?"

"I'm not selling." Ruth pushed back from the table. "I bruised my hip in a fall, Liam. I'm not one foot in the grave quite yet."

"That's not what I mean."

"It's what you've implied." She lifted herself to her feet. "Austin, will you walk me back to my bedroom?"

The boy glanced at Natalie, who nodded. "I'll clean up the kitchen, Ruth, then come back to help you dress."

"Ruth, listen—"

"No, Liam, you listen. I know you're trying to help, but pushing me into changing my whole life isn't going to happen. I've lived on my own since Stan died. I don't see any reason to change now. You keep your big mansions and private jets. I'm happy with the simple life I have here in Crimson." She leveled a look at him. "As I remember it, you were pretty happy here once upon a time. Maybe you should focus on that instead of all your high-handed plans for me."

"I didn't—"

"Come back here at six and you can take me to Saturday night bingo at Evergreen. I've got a hot streak going and I missed last weekend." She leaned on her cane. "You can join me for church tomorrow morning, as well. A little time in the pew will do your soul good."

Liam shot a look at Natalie who only shrugged. "Okay, Ruth, whatever you say."

She left the room, muttering to herself. Austin made a face at Natalie over his shoulder but she gave him a bright smile and a thumbs-up and began clearing the dishes from the table.

"I pushed her too hard."

"Ya think?" Natalie stacked plates on the counter.

"I forgot how stubborn she can be when she gets riled up."

"The fall has been hard on her. She's healing, but Ruth isn't used to depending on other people. She's a proud woman, Liam."

"I know, Nat. That's one of the things I love about her." He moved to the sink and rinsed the plates, then put them in the dishwasher. "You're a lot like her, you know." *And you both frustrate the hell out of me*, he added to himself.

After a moment, he looked up to find Natalie's eyes on him. "What are you doing?"

"Um…the dishes?"

"I didn't think big, important CEO types did their own dishes."

"Apparently the CEO card doesn't get me far in my nanny's house."

"Are you really thinking of headquartering a company in Crimson?"

Leave it to Natalie to see right through him. "Sure. If I can work out something with the town, that is. It's a good place to live and the GPS technology we're developing will appeal to people who like the outdoors. It's a natural fit."

She nodded but still looked doubtful.

They finished cleaning the kitchen in silence. There had been a lot of nights Natalie had eaten dinner over here when they were in high school. Her mom waitressed in town back then and wasn't around very often. Ruth would cook while Liam and Natalie took cleanup duty. Being here with her now brought him back to a time long past. A time his heart didn't want to forget but his brain wouldn't let him revisit.

His cell phone beeped in his pocket. "I've got some stuff to do to get settled in today."

"Before bingo?" Natalie asked, flashing him the first smile he'd seen from her.

He'd missed that smile but forced himself not to show it. "Before bingo," he agreed. "Are you okay if I head out?"

"This is my job, Liam. One of them, anyway. We're fine."

She didn't need to add "without you." He knew she'd never needed him in the same way he did her.

He nodded and turned, but stopped at the sliding door that led from the kitchen to the back of the house. "In case you were wondering, I haven't dated *gobs* of supermodels."

Her gaze crashed into his and he hoped it was relief he read in their dark depths. "It's none of my business who you date." Her words were sharp but her voice breathless.

He could see her chest rise and fall as she busied herself wiping invisible spots from the counter. It gave him the confidence to say exactly what was on his mind.

"And, Natalie?"

She looked at him again.

"No one ever compared to you. Not even close."

He watched her jaw drop as he let himself out the back door and walked away.

Chapter Two

"That's how he left it?"

"He's just cruel."

"But so dang hot."

"Why didn't you tell us your old boyfriend was hot?"

"And rich."

Natalie looked at her group of friends and licked a bit of salt from the rim of her margarita. Austin was sleeping over at a friend's house so she'd called Olivia Travers after Liam and Ruth had left for bingo and asked her friend to meet her for a drink at her favorite Mexican restaurant. She'd explained a little about the situation without giving too many details or revealing her conflicted emotions about Liam.

When she'd arrived, it was to find not only Olivia waiting, but also Olivia's sister, Millie, and their friend Katie Garrity, who owned the local bakery.

Heat crept into her cheeks. "I didn't realize this was going to be an inquisition."

Olivia looked a little guilty. "You sounded bad on the phone."

Millie held out her cell for the table to see. "I'm sure Liam Donovan could make you feel much better."

Katie took the phone and let out a low whistle. "He was cute in high school, but time has definitely been Liam's friend."

Like Natalie, Katie had been born and raised in Crimson. Olivia's husband, Logan—also a Crimson native—had come back to town, and Millie was married to Logan's oldest brother, Jake. The middle brother, Josh, also lived in Crimson, and his wife, Sara, who was currently away shooting a movie, rounded out Natalie's group of girlfriends. She'd never had close friends when she was younger and as much as she enjoyed it now, opening up to people about her private life was still difficult.

"I don't need any help from Liam." She took a drink of the sweet margarita. "He accused me of stealing from his Ruth."

"That's ridiculous," Katie said. "You work harder than anyone in town. How many jobs are you balancing right now?"

"Four if you count the jewelry business."

"It counts," Olivia answered. "Your earrings and bracelets sell better than any others in the community center gift shop."

"When are you going to branch out into other stores?" Millie asked.

"When I figure out how to function on two hours of sleep each night," Natalie answered. She loved making the jewelry she fashioned out of beads, metal and precious stones. The work both relaxed and invigorated her. The plan had always been to save enough from her nursing jobs to invest in her business so that she could expand. One more thing in her life her ex-husband had ruined.

"The point is," Katie continued, "you live simply, you work hard. I'm assuming it's to save money for Austin's college fund."

"Because it isn't your addiction to fashion," Millie interjected.

Olivia nudged her sister.

"Sorry," Millie mumbled. "Was that rude?"

"It's fine," Natalie said with a wry smile.

"Katie's right." Olivia dipped a chip into the salsa. "You're just not a big spender. Anyone who knows you would never think you'd take advantage of someone in your care."

Natalie folded and refolded her napkin. The truth was she hadn't taken Ruth's money, but she had a pretty good idea what had happened to it. She knew she needed to ask Ruth outright but was afraid of knowing the truth.

She took a deep breath and blurted, "I think Ruth might have used the money to pay off my ex-husband."

All three women stared at her. Their waitress approached the table, but Olivia shooed her away again.

"Why would Ruth need to pay off Brad Holt?" Katie asked after a moment.

"She doesn't." Natalie sighed. "She shouldn't. But I told her that he was kind of…sort of…blackmailing me, and I'm afraid she took matters into her own hands."

"Blackmailing you?" Olivia asked.

"Kind of, sort of?" Millie added.

"It's a long story."

Millie waved to the waitress. "Another round for all of us," she called. "A big plate of nachos and an order of chicken quesadillas." Luckily, the place was crowded and loud so Millie didn't draw much attention. Not that she cared. When the waitress nodded from across the restaurant, Millie gestured to Natalie. "We've got time. Go on."

"This is difficult to talk about."

Millie tapped on her own drink. "Try another sip of liquid courage."

Katie shook her head. "I don't understand why you would share something like that with one of your patients and not your friends."

Guilt flared in Natalie as she saw the hurt in her friend's gaze. "I'm sorry. I spent a lot of time with Ruth over the past several months. She needed help with some of the most basic functions. It was embarrassing for her and seemed to help when I shared details about myself. I'm normally pretty private, so it became somewhat cathartic for me. I didn't think she'd act on what I told her."

Olivia reached out a hand to pat Natalie's arm. "Tell us how it started."

"Brad and I were only married a year when he got a job doing regional sales for a company based out of Grand Junction. We'd scrimped and saved to buy a house, and I'd stopped working when Austin was born." She traced her finger along the cool condensation gathered on the side of her glass. "I was worried about money, and Brad assured me things were good. Honestly, I should have paid closer attention, but Austin was colicky. I was on my own so much. I just wanted to believe him."

Olivia nodded. "I know how that goes." Natalie remembered that Olivia's ex-husband had cheated on her before leaving her for his mistress.

"We've all made bad choices in men," Millie echoed.

Natalie glanced at Katie, who gave a slight smile. "Or no choices in men because we're too scared of making a mistake. It's no better, Nat. Trust me."

"I'm not sure you'll think that once you've heard the

whole story." She sipped her margarita, surprised to find there was nothing but ice left in the glass. The waitress slipped another one in front of her. "You're driving me home, right?" she asked Katie.

"Always," her friend answered.

Suddenly, Natalie wanted to share her embarrassing past with her friends, hoping it would help her feel not so alone. "Things were okay with us for almost a year, or so I thought. Brad traveled a lot, which made it tough for us to reconnect when he was back. I figured things would even out once Austin was a little older. I was picking up a package at the post office one day and Myrna, the old postmistress, asked me if I wanted the mail from Brad's PO box, as well. She said he hadn't collected it in months and it was taking up too much space."

She stirred the straw around in her drink. "She gave me a whole box of stuff, mainly delinquent notices and demands for payment. I can still see the pity in her eyes as she registered my shock. She must have thought I was the most gullible fool on the planet."

"I doubt that," Olivia said, her tone reassuring.

"I was pretty darn close. I took the box home, put Austin down for a nap and opened every envelope. We were months behind on the house and car payments, utilities, credit card bills, the works. At first I thought it must have been a mistake." She thumped the palm of her hand against her forehead. "Still such an idiot. We'd gotten a late notice call here or there, but Brad always explained it away. That box opened the floodgates. He'd been using his cell phone as a contact number, but I discovered things were worse than I could have imagined."

"And was he able to explain it away?" Millie asked, her tone dripping with sarcasm.

"Actually, I think he was relieved to finally be caught,"

Natalie admitted. "As soon as I knew, all the debts became my responsibility. He was off the hook once more."

"Was it drugs?" Katie asked.

"Not really." Natalie shook her head. "Maybe some dabbling but nothing hard-core. I lost count of his vices. Gambling was his main addiction. Most of the work he did was in Arizona and Nevada. He got sucked into the Vegas culture and couldn't find a way out."

Millie narrowed her eyes. "Tell me you aren't making excuses for him."

"Not at all. He cost us everything. My car was repossessed, the house was almost foreclosed on and our credit destroyed. It's only in the past couple of years that I've felt comfortable answering the phone to an unknown number. I had creditors hounding me for so long."

"Why you? It was Brad's gambling."

"Everything was in both our names. I could either pay off the debts or file for bankruptcy."

"Oh, sweetie." Katie got up and came around the table to wrap her arms around Natalie's shoulders. "Why didn't you tell anyone? We could have helped."

"I was too embarrassed. It feels silly to say that now, but it's the truth."

"So that's when you left him?" Olivia asked.

Natalie nodded. "I gave him an ultimatum. Go to rehab for his addiction or I was leaving. He told me he'd change but was unwilling to get professional help. I filed for divorce within a month of discovering what he'd done."

Katie sat down again. "I don't understand why you think Ruth would pay him off now. You've been divorced for almost eight years."

"At the time, I wanted him out of our lives until he could get control of things again. I was angry, hurt and scared. Jason Crenshaw was my attorney for the divorce. He begged me to go after Brad for full custody, to reveal everything Brad had done to wreck our finances, but I didn't want to air my dirty laundry in front of the whole town. Being a single mother seemed to hold enough stigma."

"Because of how your mom was treated when she returned to Crimson?"

"I guess," Natalie said with a shrug. "She's definitely had a chip on her shoulders for a lot of years. You know she still has a tendency to go off the rails. I couldn't handle everyone thinking I was like her in any way. The bottom line was I didn't listen to Jase. I told him to make the conditions of the divorce fair to both of us, to give Brad the option of visitation when and if he straightened out his life."

She leaned forward and took a long drink from her straw. "As a result, whenever Brad runs out of money, he comes to me making veiled threats about getting back into Austin's life. If I thought he really meant it, I'd welcome him. No boy should have to grow up without a dad around. But it's all about the money every single time. As soon as I offer it to him, he takes off again."

"Scumbag," Katie mumbled. Olivia and Millie nodded in agreement.

"Things have gotten worse in the past year. He's racked up a lot of debt again. He's telling the guys holding most of his loans that he helps me out financially, letting them think that's why he can't pay. I've given him as much as I can spare, but it isn't enough."

Olivia's mouth dropped. "Natalie, this is serious."

"I know it's serious."

"You have to go to the police."

"And Jase," Katie added. "Take legal action against Brad. File a restraining order. Whatever you need to do."

"What happens when he wants to see Austin again? I can't legally keep him from that."

Katie shook her head. "Have you talked to Jase? He's a good attorney and now that he's on town council, he has a lot of pull around here. He could help you."

"I'd planned to, but I didn't think it would get this far. I gave Brad everything I'd saved almost seven months ago and told him that was the end. Then he started calling again. That's when I told Ruth what was going on. I'm afraid she's taken matters into her own hands. She's got strangely good connections for someone her age."

"Did you ask her?"

As her stomach pitched, Natalie gripped the stem of her margarita glass. "I only realized it when Liam accused me of taking the money. She kept Austin at her side most of the day yesterday. She's definitely avoiding me. Once I know for sure I'm going to have to tell Liam. How humiliating is it to admit to the guy who left me behind that I've royally messed up my life?"

"You didn't mess it up. The scumbag ex-husband messed it up," Millie offered sympathetically.

"I married him."

Millie lifted her glass in a mock toast. "Good point."

"I have money from the inheritance I got when my grandma died," Katie offered. "I can help you pay back Ruth if she did indeed give money to Brad."

Natalie shook her head. "As much as I appreciate the offer, I need to take care of this mess myself. I know I have to stand up to Brad so this stops. It's no way to live." She took a bite of the chicken quesadilla wedge Olivia put on her plate. "It's not fair to Austin. I'm always struggling to get ahead and I should be putting money away for his college. He deserves so much more than I'm giving him right now."

"You deserve more, too," Olivia reminded her.

Fear and guilt warred inside her. Her ex-husband was a problem that had been growing for years, like a festering wound she continued to try to hide with a Band-Aid. As worried as it made her, she had to deal with him, no matter the fallout. "I'm going to talk to Ruth and if she did give money to Brad, I'll figure out how to pay her back."

"And?" Katie prompted.

"And ask Jason Crenshaw about getting the terms of the divorce redone. It will mean going back to court, but if Brad tries to fight me I'll go public with everything. I'll press charges if I have to."

"Attagirl," Millie told her.

"Whatever happens," Katie added, "you're not alone. You have friends and we're here for you, Natalie."

"Thank you." Natalie blinked several times. She was a lot of things, but a crier wasn't one of them.

"Your mother?" Katie asked. "How much does she know?"

"Very little. Mom was always very pro-Brad. She thought if I'd managed to catch a husband, that my main job was to keep him happy. She was furious when Brad and I divorced. I tried to explain the situation to her then, but she didn't want to hear it." She took a deep breath. "I guess it's time to try again."

"What about Liam?"

Natalie thought about Liam's stormy eyes and the way her whole body tingled when he towered over her. "I'm hoping to have everything sorted out with Ruth before Liam has to know any details."

"You two were close once," Katie said gently. "He's rich and powerful. He could make a good ally."

"No way. Liam made it clear what he thought of me when he left Crimson for college. He walked away and never looked back. As far as he will ever know, staying in town only brought me happiness."

Her friends looked skeptical but didn't argue with her.

"Whatever you need, we're here," Katie said. "Promise you won't go forward alone."

Natalie gave a jerky nod and wiped her fingers across her cheeks. "I'm going to make this right." She just hoped she could do it before her life blew up any more than it already had.

Liam walked out the front door of Ruth's house later that night, rubbing his hand along the back of his neck. He'd brought her home after she won several rounds of bingo. He'd promptly fallen asleep in her bedroom's big recliner as they watched reruns of *I Love Lucy*. She was fast asleep when he'd woken up a few minutes ago.

It was almost midnight as he pulled his phone out of his coat pocket. Several texts had come through from his latest ex-girlfriend, asking to see him again. Gretchen had called herself his girlfriend, although they'd only dated a couple of weeks before he'd ended things. Liam hadn't allowed himself to have a serious girlfriend since—well, since Natalie had chosen Crimson over him.

Seeing her boy had been like a swift kick to the gut for Liam. Long ago, he'd imagined himself as the father of Natalie's children. Those days seemed like a lifetime ago. He looked over his shoulder at the dark house. Liam's chest tightened at the thought of Natalie curled up asleep inside. He tipped back his head, marveling at the amount of stars in the sky above him even as his lungs burned from the frosty air. He'd forgotten that about Crimson, both the hollow cold of night and how clear the sky could be without the city lights in the distance.

As he turned for his SUV, he noticed a light on in the

workshop that sat at the barn across the driveway. He started toward it, then noticed a woman's frame silhouetted in the window. Natalie.

He watched her for several minutes, her hair pulled back in a messy bun and wearing a faded chambray shirt rolled up to her elbows. Memory sparked in his mind, and he smiled as he headed for the door to the barn's workshop.

Natalie didn't notice him come in and he realized she had earbuds in her ears as she hummed softly along with music he couldn't hear. She held a pair of needle-nose pliers in one hand as she twisted a thin wire held under a bright light. After a moment, she reached for a bead from a case in front of her. She glanced up, and her gaze crashed into his.

She screamed, slapping one hand to her chest as the earbuds ripped out of her ears. Her fingers upended the jar of beads, which went flying in all directions.

"Sorry," Liam said, although he wasn't sorry to not be the only one in the room with a racing heart, even if it was for an entirely different reason. "I didn't mean to scare you." That much was true.

"What are you still doing here?"

"I fell asleep watching TV with Ruth. Someone put a blanket over me."

She took several deep breaths, her chest rising and falling in a way that made his mouth go dry. "I check on her before I go to bed each night."

"You're not in bed."

"So observant, Liam."

"And you're wearing my shirt."

At this, her gaze dropped. "Was this old thing yours?" She wrapped her arms around her waist. "I'd forgotten."

He didn't bother to call her out on the lie. "It was my favorite."

"Want it back?"

"It looks better on you." He crouched down and began collecting the scattered beads from the floor. "As I remember, most of my clothes did."

She also picked up beads, and Liam found the silence oddly companionable. That was until the waistband of her jeans slipped down her hips and he got a flash of creamy skin again. He forced his thoughts away from her and focused only on reaching for the last of the beads.

But as he came around the table and straightened, he found himself directly in front of Natalie. She stood totally still, her hand holding steady the bowl of beads. He dropped the ones he'd collected in and interlaced his fingers with hers, drawing his thumb along the calluses on the pads of her fingers.

"How long have you made jewelry?"

"A few years now," she whispered with a self-deprecating smile. "I don't sleep much and it relaxes me."

"You have talent."

"It's just for fun."

He let out a bark of laughter. "I don't believe that for a minute. When was the last time you did something just for fun?"

Her mouth tightened as she looked deep into his eyes. "You were the last thing I did just for fun, Liam."

Despite how wrong it was, he wanted to be that for her again. He smoothed back the hair from her face and leaned forward. She closed her eyes, but instead of taking her mouth the way he wanted, he kissed the edge of her lips, then the tiny birthmark on the side of her temple. Her skin was as soft as he remembered, and she smelled like everything that had ever been good in his life.

When she turned her face toward his, he couldn't resist anymore. He claimed her mouth, gently exploring her with his lips and tongue. She opened for him and he delved in, reveling in the feel of her in his arms once again.

Before things became too heated, she pulled away. Liam nearly groaned, but he took a step back. One thing he knew for certain about Natalie was that if he pushed too hard and too quickly, she'd only retreat further.

"My life isn't simple anymore," she said quietly.

"I don't want to be a complication."

She took a breath and raised her hand as if to touch him before pulling away. "I think I know what happened to Ruth's money."

He stiffened.

"I didn't take it. I promise."

"Tell me everything."

She shook her head. "I can't until I know for sure."

"What the hell does that mean?"

"It means you'll have to trust me." She dropped her gaze to the floor, then back to him. "Please, Liam."

Trust her? The last time Liam trusted Natalie it had been with his heart, and it ended up crushed into a million pieces. But in the quiet of this evening, he didn't want to fight. Right now he remembered all the reasons he'd first been attracted to her, how she'd pulled him to her in a way no woman had before or since.

"I've rented a house outside of town for a month. You have that much time to get this figured out, but you have to promise me that no more of Ruth's money will go missing in the meantime."

She gave a small nod. "Don't you usually stay in Aspen when you visit?"

So she had kept track of him, at least a tiny bit. The

knowledge gave him a rush. He'd always stayed in the nearby town using the excuse that it was more to his taste than homey, quaint Crimson. The real reason was standing in front of him. He had never trusted himself to be so close to Natalie, hadn't wanted to chance running into her around town. Now he realized how foolish that had been. Even if she wasn't standing in front of him, she had never been far from his mind, no matter what he'd told himself.

"I wanted to be closer on this trip. If she weren't so stubborn, I'd have her living with me now. Or in the room at Evergreen I get billed for every month."

"I thought you knew about her arrangement there. Really I did. But she loves this place. It's her home."

He shook his head. "I've never understood the concept of home."

"What do your parents think of you looking at Crimson as a headquarters for the new company?" She bit down on her lower lip as she waited for his answer, a gesture of concern he recognized from long ago.

It took him a minute to follow her words, as her teeth tugging against that full mouth distracted him. "I haven't mentioned it to them."

"They won't like it."

"This company is mine," he told her. "It's none of my parents' business where I locate it."

"You've had a lot of success, Liam. You've accomplished so much in the past ten years."

"Have you kept track of my career, Nat?" The thought gave him another jolt of adrenaline.

"We do get news in Crimson. Donovan Enterprises is kind of a big deal. A Fortune 500 software company."

It was also the company his father had founded, and Liam was reminded every day that he was lucky to be riding the family coattails. Even when the innovations and products he'd spearheaded had led to much of the company's recent success. That's why this new venture was so important to him and why his father didn't know anything about it.

"Plus Ruth brags about you to anyone who will listen."

"She does?"

"Ruth is very proud of you. Being your nanny, helping to raise you, was special to her. I'm sure she's going to take full credit for convincing you to bring more jobs to Crimson."

That got his attention and not in a good way. "I said I'm considering Crimson," he clarified. "Nothing is decided yet."

"I know." She smiled. "She'll take credit anyway."

"You really care about her?"

She nodded. "Of course. She's a wonderful person." Her smile faded. "My relationship with my mother has never been great. It means a lot to me, and to Austin, to have someone like Ruth in our lives."

She was right, of course. His nanny had been a huge bright spot in his life when he was a kid, even if he hadn't appreciated it at the time. She'd helped raise his father then come back to work for his parents when Liam was six. Even as a young kid, his mom and dad hadn't had time for him. Ruth always had. A little voice inside him said Natalie might fall into the same category, but he silenced it before he had no choice but to listen.

He took a step back and forced himself to focus on why he'd come to Crimson in the first place. "I'm here for Ruth, Natalie. I'll give you time because she seems to trust you. But she's my priority. I won't let anyone take advantage of her and I'll do whatever is necessary to make sure she's okay. Remember that."

Her gaze shuttered and Liam cursed himself for pushing her away so quickly, even when he knew it was the right thing to do.

"Got it." She gave him a mock salute. "I'm expendable if it comes to that. Nothing much has changed on that front, so I won't get confused." She turned back to her worktable. "I work an afternoon shift at Evergreen tomorrow. If you want to be here while I'm gone, Ruth would appreciate the company. Otherwise, I can take her with me."

All superficial business. That's what he wanted from his relationship with Natalie, so why did it irritate him to have her speak so curtly? "I'll be here," he answered, unwilling to give away his feelings. If she could shut him out so easily, he could do the same.

"Good night, Liam." Her hand reached out for the pliers once again. Liam wondered if he imagined the slight tremble in her fingers.

She was dismissing him, much like she'd done back in high school. Fine. He couldn't care less. He turned, forcing himself not to look back at her, and walked out into the night.

Chapter Three

Liam was up for an early run Monday morning despite the layer of frost and temperature that made his lungs burn. The way he was huffing air as he got back to the house he'd rented reminded him that Crimson sat at an almost nine-thousand-foot altitude, tucked high into the Rocky Mountains of Colorado.

He'd acclimate within a few days, he told himself as he came into the large, modern kitchen overlooking the valley below. Sun bounced off the snow that blanketed the trees and mountainside, almost blinding in its brightness. It looked like a picture postcard for a winter wonderland. He wiped his forehead on the back of his jacket sleeve and reached for a bottle of water from the refrigerator.

"I made coffee," a voice said from behind him.

"You still on central time, too?" He turned to his assistant, Tanner Black, who was frowning at the screen of a laptop he carried into the room.

Tanner was a few years older than Liam and had been

his right-hand man for almost four years. Liam's father had a habit of taking his bad moods out on the people who worked for him. The first time Liam had seen Tanner, the other man had intervened when Michael Donovan was in the midst of a tirade that had brought a young secretary to tears. Who knew what the woman had done—not gotten Michael's coffee order exactly right, answered the phone on the third ring instead of the second. When Michael went off, nothing rational seemed to matter.

Liam had been about to step in when Tanner, a junior project manager at the company, had come forward and given Liam's father a stern lecture in his no-nonsense way. Tanner had been fired on the spot, but Liam had re-hired him just as quickly. He knew how valuable it would prove to have someone in his corner who wasn't afraid of Michael Donovan.

Tanner had quickly become indispensable to Liam. He was a great project manager, a forward thinker and one of the few people in the company Liam trusted implicitly. He'd helped every step of the way with the new company and understood why Liam needed to break off from the "father ship," as he referred to Donovan Enterprises.

"Sleep is overrated." Tanner placed the computer on the counter and filled a mug with coffee. He wore a charcoal-gray suit with a tailored shirt and red tie. Even in the mountains, Tanner insisted on dressing for business. "All things are possible with enough coffee as fuel. Don't forget the Skype meeting today with the investors. You need to lock these guys up so we can move forward with a development plan for the new app."

Liam nodded. "No problem. They won't want to miss this opportunity."

"Because your father pushed them out before the last stock split at Donovan Enterprises?"

"That's one of several reasons."

Tanner lifted a blond brow. "Do you have a plan for breaking the news to dear old dad?"

"Not yet." Liam grabbed a muffin from the box on the counter and bit into it, the texture moist and the flavor out of this world. He looked at the name imprinted on the box, Life is Sweet. He remembered the small downtown bakery from his time in Crimson but didn't remember the shop offering anything like this.

"It's good, right?" Tanner asked with a smile. "You should try one of her cookies. I half fell in love with the woman who runs the place because of the way she bakes."

"And…" Liam prompted.

"And it doesn't hurt that she's gorgeous."

If Liam had a quarter for all the women Tanner "half fell in love with," he'd have the money to fund his new company all on his own.

"Why didn't you tell me Crimson was such a great town? Whenever we were in Aspen, you went out of your way not to spend time here." Tanner snagged a muffin. "I think it has a great vibe."

"Good," Liam answered, "because I want you to look into headquartering the new company here."

Tanner's mouth dropped open. "I meant a great vibe for a weekend away. You can't be serious."

"Why not? I bet the town will offer incentives, the location will attract the kind of people we want working on the GPS software and it keeps us far away from Donovan Enterprises."

"And…" Tanner used the same tone Liam had a few minutes earlier.

"And I told my nanny part of why I was staying in town was because I might start the company here."

"Bold move." Tanner broke off a piece of muffin and popped it into his mouth. "Are you serious?"

"I'm serious about making her believe it could happen." Liam took a long drink of coffee, not wanting to admit how much the idea of once again calling Crimson his home appealed to him.

"Got it. How was bingo?" Tanner asked with a smile.

"A rocking good time." Liam spun the laptop around and logged into his email.

"Is there anything more you want me to check out regarding where your nanny is spending her money or who's taking it?"

Natalie's soft "please" came to Liam's mind, along with her big melted-chocolate eyes. Eyes that were haunted and hiding something. "Not yet." He let out a small laugh as he checked his in-box for new messages. "I'll be damned, word does travel fast from the bingo hall."

"Can you translate that sentence into English?" Tanner asked, pouring himself more coffee.

"What time is the investor call?"

"Noon eastern time."

Liam nodded, flipping the laptop shut. "I'm going to have breakfast with one of the Crimson town council members. He wants to talk about my plans for headquartering LifeMap here."

Tanner whistled. "Are there any secrets in Crimson?"

"Sure," Liam answered as he walked toward the master suite. "They just don't stay secrets for long."

He walked into a homey restaurant near the center of town a half hour later, trying to ignore the excessive amount of holiday decorations strewn up and down Main Street. Or maybe they just felt excessive to Liam. He'd never been a fan of Christmas, but Crimson clearly embraced the holiday with lights and garland strung between shops and ornaments and other trimmings hanging from every window.

He looked around the oversize Christmas tree at the front of the restaurant to see Jason Crenshaw at one of the side tables. Jase had been one of the first kids Liam had met when he came to Crimson in high school. Back then, Jase was tall and lanky, a little on the nerdy side, a straight-A student and president of almost every club at the school.

Liam had liked him a lot, but at that point in his life, he was more interested in getting in trouble to hack off his parents than getting good grades, so he and Jase had gone in different directions.

Jase stood as Liam approached and reached out his hand for a hearty shake. He was still tall, at least a couple of inches over Liam's own six-two, but he'd filled out and looked every inch the perfect representative for a town like Crimson.

Almost immediately, an older waitress came over with a coffeepot. "Drive over from Aspen, hon?" she asked, pouring steaming liquid into Liam's mug then freshening Jase's cup.

Liam glanced between the waitress and Jase, who shrugged. "I'm staying in Crimson," he answered.

"Is that right? I didn't mean any offense. But we're a beer and burgers town. You look more the steak and fancy wine type."

"I like beer," Liam muttered, wondering why the woman's assessment of him grated on his nerves. He'd put on a button-down shirt, black trousers and a dark leather jacket for this meeting, and as far as he could tell he didn't look much different from Jase.

"Ruth Keller was Liam's nanny for years," Jase told the waitress.

Her eyes lit up. "The one bringing all the jobs to Crimson?" She gave him a maternal pat on the shoulder. "Breakfast is on the house for you."

"That isn't necessary," Liam answered quickly. "I haven't made a final decision. There's a lot that goes into—"

"So you're not starting your company here?"

Jase shook his head but smiled. "Let's not jump the gun, Mary. We're meeting this morning to discuss the possibility. It's great they're even considering Crimson." He tapped his menu. "I'll have the breakfast burrito with green chili, hash browns on the side."

The waitress nodded and turned to Liam.

"I'll have the same."

She leaned toward Jase. "Do I buy him breakfast now or later?" she asked in a whisper that Liam could clearly hear.

"I'll take care of the bill this morning," Jase answered.

Satisfied with that answer, she turned from their table.

"Is there some kind of news alert in this town that everyone subscribes to?" Liam asked when she was out of earshot. "I've never seen something spread so quickly."

"That's Crimson for you." Jase dumped a packet of sugar into his coffee. "Even if you don't know your own business, chances are someone else can fill you in on the details."

"How do you stand it?" As much as he was in the public eye for his job, Liam liked to keep his private dealings close to the vest. That seemed impossible in a town like Crimson.

Jase shrugged. "Keep my nose clean for one. I also

know that people have good intentions for the most part. You get used to it."

"You've done well here." Liam stirred creamer into his coffee. "Of course, I think you would have done well anywhere from what I remember about your track record in high school."

"Crimson is home for me. Always has been." Jase watched Liam over the rim of his coffee mug. "I have to say I'm surprised to hear you're in town for an extended stay."

"I want to make sure Ruth gets the care she needs. She doesn't have any family of her own."

"Makes sense," Jase said with a nod. "She talks about you like you're her own flesh and blood. Are you really considering Crimson as a company headquarters?"

Liam looked around the restaurant before answering. There was a mix of customers, from families with young children, to a couple of tables of older folks, to men clearly dressed for a day on the slopes. The mood was friendly and open, much like he'd found throughout the town. His feelings about Crimson from years ago were jumbled, but he couldn't deny that the present-day atmosphere was appealing.

"If we can make it work, I'd give it a go. But you should know this new company has nothing to do with Donovan Enterprises. My father and his money won't be involved. I don't know if that impacts your interest in us." He watched Jase closely, waited for the disappointment that his father wasn't backing LifeMap to flicker across the other man's face. When it didn't, Liam felt the tension ease out of his shoulders. "I'm courting investors now and hope to have financing secured by the end of the month. That's another reason I'm in Crimson. The guys who own the venture capital company we've been working with are coming to

Aspen to ski in a couple of weeks. I hope to meet with them in a more relaxed setting and close the deal."

"If the deal means jobs and revenue for Crimson, I'm all for it. It's not a sure thing on the town's end, though. There are a couple of old-school locals on the council. They'd like to see Crimson revert back to how things were in the fifties—one stop sign in the middle of town and all that. But several of us have other ideas for the future of the town." He leaned closer. "You should also know I'm planning on running for mayor next year."

"This would be a damn good feather in your campaign cap."

The waitress brought their plates at that moment. "Hope you like your green chili hot," she said to Liam as she slid a dish with a football-size burrito smothered in green sauce in front of him. "We do things spicy here in Crimson."

He couldn't help but return her grin. "I like it spicy," he answered with a wink.

She laughed. "You'll fit in here, hon. Even if you do look like a smooth talker."

Liam shook his head. "You have an uncanny ability to compliment and criticize in the same breath. That's quite a skill."

"Thank you, sweetness. I pride myself on it."

"I love this town," Jase said when she'd walked away again. He forked up a big bite of burrito. "It's my home. Yes, I want to win my bid for mayor, but even more I want what's best for Crimson." He pointed the utensil at Liam. "If this deal works out, are you planning on sticking around longer?"

Liam took a bite of his own burrito as a way to buy himself a little time to think about his answer to that question. The idea of headquartering his new company here was just something he'd thrown out to appease his former nanny. Two days ago, he'd had no intention of spending more time in this town than was absolutely necessary. He had to admit the thought of starting LifeMap here held some appeal, even beyond making his father furious. But he couldn't quite forget the past or how badly things had ended for him in Crimson once before. Although his anger and resentment felt as though they'd gone through a process to dull them, take down the harsh edges. He reached for the pain but couldn't quite grasp it.

What he could remember with great detail was the way Natalie had felt in his arms last night. "There's a long way to go before any decisions are made. I hadn't really planned on considering Crimson as a headquarters, so we have other locations in the running, as well. I'm willing to consider this town if it can offer what we need."

"What exactly is it you need, Liam?"

The word *home* popped immediately into Liam's mind. A place where he was more than just his last name or his bank account. He focused instead on the company. "LifeMap needs to attract talented, smart people. I'm going to need a team of programmers as well as marketing experts. I want to invest good money in my intellectual capital and build a company that will attract those kinds of employees. The location will be important and I'd rather not do a new build. If I can renovate something or find a spot that's move-in ready I'd be thrilled. That's where you're at a disadvantage. Bigger cities have a lot more to offer."

"I can set you up with a commercial Realtor later today. If this moves forward, we can start talking about incentives from the town. We're small, but we mean business." He took another sip of coffee. "If you need a contractor to oversee renovations, they don't get any better than Logan Travers. He came back to town last year and focuses mainly on residential and historic buildings downtown, but I'm sure he could give you some great advice. Do you remember him?"

Liam felt his breath hitch as his chest constricted. "Of course I remember Logan," he said, his voice raspy. "His twin sister died in my arms."

Chapter Four

"If you take the medicine without a fuss, Mr. Manzia, I'll give you an extra scoop of ice cream."

"It tastes bad," the older man said with a shake of his head, turning back to his newspaper.

Natalie wanted to groan. She was six hours into her shift and had a headache to match. Harold Manzia always complained about medicine. Normally she took it in stride, playing little games to see how quickly she could get him to acquiesce. But since her encounter with Liam two nights ago, she'd been sleeping worse than usual and was not on top of her game today.

"Harold, would you walk me down to the community room?" Ruth looked up from her needlework. "I'd like to get a good seat for the children's concert this afternoon." She gave Natalie a slow wink as Harold tossed down the paper and came to his feet.

"Be happy to, Ruthie." It was no secret the elderly widower had quite a crush on Ruth.

"Medicine first," Natalie said, holding out the small plastic cup of liquid.

Harold waved her away. "Later."

Natalie moved in front of Harold. "Now."

"I'm sure one of the other men would be able to take me if you can't." Ruth glanced over her shoulder. "But I was looking forward to spending the afternoon with you."

With a growl, Harold grabbed the cup from Natalie and downed the white liquid, only shuddering a little as he did. "Nasty stuff."

"I know," Natalie conceded as he handed her the empty vial. "But it keeps you regular."

"Regular is good," Ruth added. "George Clark gets the worst gas when things aren't moving. I can barely stand to be around him." She stood, then reached out to pat Harold's fingers. "I wouldn't want that to happen to you, Harold."

Natalie suppressed a smile as Mr. Manzia considered the possibility. She pressed a quick kiss to Ruth's temple. "Thanks for the help."

"My pleasure, dear," Ruth whispered.

"About what I asked you earlier—your money and my ex-husband…"

Ruth's sharp gaze went suddenly blank. "Liam handles my money, Natalie. You know he has gobs."

"Yes, but—"

"It was such a shame the two of you broke up. Now that he's back in town, maybe there's another chance. He might ask you to the winter dance at the high school."

"We've been out of high school for over ten years, Ruth. You remember that, right?"

"Oh, well…" Ruth closed her eyes for a moment, then opened them and smiled. "He'll buy you the loveliest corsage."

Natalie bit back a sigh as Harold stepped forward. "Ready, Ruthie?"

"Harold really is my favorite," Ruth told Natalie before turning to the older man.

Natalie watched as Harold took Ruth's arm and headed toward the hall. The music teacher at Austin's elementary school had arranged for the kids in his class to come to Evergreen and sing Christmas carols to the residents. As soon as Natalie finished a few charts, she'd join them for the performance.

When she turned for the nurses' office, Liam was standing in the doorway. Heat flooded through her at the sight of him and she had to force herself not to fidget. "You just missed Ruth," she said, tossing Harold's empty cup into a nearby trash can, then refolding the newspaper. She wondered how much of the conversation he'd overheard.

"I noticed." He leaned a shoulder against the door frame, unzipping his insulated jacket. For some reason, the soft colors of the senior center made him look even more rugged in comparison. Not that Natalie was paying attention. "She always had a way with the men."

"Why do you think she never remarried after her husband died?"

Liam shrugged. "She always said she might have a lot of love *in* her life but there had only ever been one love *of* her life." The way he stared at her as he said the words made a shiver run across the back of her neck. "Does she often come with you to the center during the day?"

"A couple of times a week before her fall." Natalie fluffed a pillow on the sofa in the now-empty sitting room. Residents loved when kids came to visit, so people who would normally be gathered around the television or playing games in the dining hall had gone down to the community room for the concert. "Her other nurse called in sick today and I didn't want to leave her at the house alone."

"You could have called me."

There was something in his tone, maybe accusation, and her defenses pricked in response. "She's hired me to be her nurse. If I thought there was an issue with her leaving the house I wouldn't have brought her. I'm good at what I do, Liam."

"I'm not arguing that, but she's like family to me."

He probably hadn't meant the comment as an intentional barb, but it still stung. Nothing would have made Natalie happier than to have Ruth as part of her real family. "And I'm the hired help. I get it."

She went to walk past him but stopped when he grabbed her arm. "I didn't mean it like that, Nat. I want to take care of her. Hell, I could hire private nurses around the clock to be with her."

"That's not what she wants."

"But is it what she needs?" He squeezed her arm tighter for a moment then released it again. "She's aged so much since I've seen her last. It makes me feel like a jackass for letting things…for not coming back to Crimson sooner."

"You're busy. She understands that."

"I shouldn't be too busy for her. She's the only person who ever really cared about me. She didn't have to take me in when I got kicked out of boarding school. My parents would have been happy to ship me off to a military academy for the last part of high school if she hadn't intervened. Living with her in Crimson was one of the best times in my life." A shadow crossed his face and suddenly he looked less like the powerful CEO he was now and more like the vulnerable boy she remembered. The boy she'd fallen in love with all those years ago.

She leaned closer, drawn as always to him. Close enough that she could see the dusting of stubble across his jaw and the faint shadows under his eyes. Maybe she wasn't the only one having trouble sleeping. The thought of Liam stretched across his bed made another rush of heat climb her face. She took a quick step back to break the spell, the connection between them that renewed itself so quickly.

"Do you have time for a concert?" she asked, pulling at the hem of her scrub shirt, needing something to do with her fingers to stop herself from reaching for him.

"Concert?" he repeated, blinking several times.

"My son's class is performing here this afternoon. Holiday songs mostly." She realized how lame her invitation sounded. Liam Donovan ran a multinational corporation. He didn't have time for grade-school musicals.

"I'd love to," he answered.

She gave a sharp nod in response. Why had she made the offer? The less time she spent in Liam's company, the better for her sanity. "Let me just check on a couple of the other residents and I'll walk down with you."

"I'll be here." Liam smiled and her mind went blank. She remembered that same feeling from high school. The weeks after he'd first arrived, before she'd known him, she'd spent stealing glances, hoping to catch his gaze, then too embarrassed to hold it when she had. It was like that even now. After several moments, his eyebrow lifted. "The residents?"

"Right." Mortified, she turned and fled into one of the rooms off the hall. She took more time than she needed, especially since the few residents left on the hall were resting. Part of her hoped Liam would get tired of waiting for her and she'd have a few extra minutes to get her emotions in check. Even after ten years, he had the ability to unnerve her, and Natalie craved control. She made sure the other nurse on duty knew she was heading down to the community room, then peeked back into the common area. Liam stood facing the far wall, examining the resident artwork hanging there.

"We have a local artist come in to teach a painting class."

"Some of them are quite good," he said, turning to her.

"More importantly, they all enjoy it. Evergreen offers a variety of enrichment activities. Even if she doesn't stay here, we make sure Ruth has access to everything."

He slid her a look. "She's in good hands. I'm sorry if I insinuated anything else."

She led the way down the hall. "This is my job, but I feel a personal connection to every one of my patients." Her voice lowered. "Especially your nanny. She's been good to Austin and me. I owe her a lot."

His step faltered and Natalie found herself blushing again. Was he thinking of how he'd accused her of stealing money from Ruth? She'd tried to talk to Ruth while Austin was brushing his teeth this morning, but the older woman had an uncanny ability to turn forgetful when she didn't want to discuss a certain subject. Natalie didn't know whether Ruth did it on purpose, or her memory truly failed when she became agitated. Natalie wanted to be sure Brad wasn't involved so she could reassure Liam that the missing money had nothing to do with her.

"She's happy you're here," she went on quickly, realizing he was staring at her. "I know she's missed you."

"What about you, Nat? Do you ever miss me?"

* * *

As soon as the words were out of his mouth, Liam regretted them. He wanted to know that she'd missed him—that she'd spent as many moments remembering their time together as he had. He was scared to death she hadn't.

She opened her mouth to answer just as a small voice cried out, "Mom, over here."

Natalie whirled to where a row of kids lined the hallway wall. Her son was waving furiously, almost jumping up and down with excitement. She glanced back at Liam, her gaze unreadable.

"Pretend I never asked the question," he said quickly.

Her mouth quirked. "As if."

"Mom!"

She walked over to Austin, then bent at the knee to look him in the eye. Liam couldn't hear what she said but the boy's face lit up, his smile wide. As Austin threw his arms around his mom, Liam's chest tightened. Of course Natalie was an amazing mother. For all her tough exterior, she was one of the most nurturing people he'd ever met. She had that in common with his former nanny.

He slipped into the community room, spotting Ruth near the front. She waved, pointing to a row of empty chairs along the wall. He grabbed one and pushed it close. "Don't you love the holidays?" she whispered as he sat, her eyes glowing as bright as Austin's. "I'm so happy to have you with me."

"Me, too." He cleared his throat when his voice caught on the words. He shrugged out of his coat, suddenly warm in the crowded room. As the schoolchildren filed in and up onto the risers set at the front, Ruth reached over and took his hand in hers. Her skin felt paper-thin, her fingers cool and fragile wrapped around his. How had she aged so much in the couple of years since he'd last visited? He knew the fall had taken a lot out of her. The doctor had told him she was lucky she hadn't broken any bones.

A teacher stepped to the front and introduced the third grade class from Crimson Creek Elementary. The kids launched into a rendition of "Rudolph, the Red-Nosed Reindeer" that was more energetic than harmonious, but it didn't seem to matter. The audience loved the kids' enthusiasm and many of them sang along with the well-known carols. When one of the boys came forward for a whisper-soft solo of "Silent Night," Liam saw Ruth wipe a tear from the corner of her eye.

It made him remember how much she'd always loved the holidays. During the time he'd lived with her, they'd gone into the woods together to cut down a fresh Christmas tree, then decorated it with a mix of homemade and sparkling new ornaments. She'd had him help her bake cookies and string lights, adding more spirit to his holidays than he'd ever had with his parents. His father's idea of a perfect Christmas was spending the week at an exclusive beach resort. There might be decorations but never of the homey, personal kind he associated with Crimson.

Looking over at his former nanny's shining eyes, the kids dressed in various shades of red and green, Liam realized he hadn't seen one decoration on display at her house. It was only the first week of December, but usually she had her Christmas tree up even before Thanksgiving. He decided at that moment that he'd make up for lost time and give her the best, most festive holiday she'd ever seen. It certainly wouldn't hurt that Natalie would be a part of it.

The kids sang several more songs, each greeted with rousing applause from the audience. At the end of the performance, the director of the assisted living center announced a cookies and juice reception in the dining hall next door. As the children followed their teacher from the room, Austin slipped out of the line and ran over to give Ruth a hug. She dropped Liam's hand to wrap her arms around the boy.

"You sounded beautiful," she told him, and his smile widened.

"I'll save you a cookie," he said and joined the back of his class.

"He really feels connected to you." Liam stood and offered his arm as he walked her toward the door.

"He keeps me young," she answered, patting his hand. It was a slow procession toward the dining hall, especially with Ruth's cane. "I should be done with this thing in a week, after my next appointment."

"Are you sure you won't come and stay with me if you don't want to live at Evergreen?" Liam led her around the corner. "There's a whole suite on the first floor of the house. I can set it up however you want."

"I'm not leaving the farm, Liam."

"It worries me to have you there by yourself."

"I'm not by myself. Natalie and Austin are there."

"You know what I mean."

She put her hand on the doorway to the dining hall to stop their progress and turned to him. "I've lived in that house for over twenty years. Stan and I dreamed of growing old together on the farm. He took his last breath on that property the year before you came to live with me. I made a promise to him that I'd create for myself in Crimson the life we'd imagined together, and I have. I won't give it up. I may be older and slower, but I'm strong enough to honor his memory."

Her eyes shone as she spoke the words. How was Liam

supposed to argue? He nodded instead. "If it's okay with you, I'm going to stay in town through the holidays."

"It's more than okay, sweetie. It would make this the best Christmas I've had in a long time." She inched forward, leaned her cane near the edge of the doorway. "Now help me to the refreshment table. I'm sick of holding that thing."

"Are you sure?" He stepped in front of her. "Should we check with Natalie or a doctor?"

She narrowed her eyes at him for a moment. "Natalie's a saint but I don't need her or a doctor to tell me how much my body can handle."

"If you get me in trouble with Natalie over this, you'll have to look for another partner in crime."

She laughed, taking his arm to slowly walk into the dining hall. "You've been in hot water with that girl since the day you left town. Maybe it's about time you fixed it."

If only he knew how. Luckily he was saved from answering when several people approached them. Ruth made introductions and Liam was barely surprised when her friends had more details about his company and the possibility of its headquarters in Crimson than he did.

They made their way toward the table set with punch and plates of cookies. As he'd promised, Austin was waiting with a chocolate cookie wrapped in a napkin. Natalie stood next to him, speaking with one of the other nurses. Her scrubs were shapeless, with images of puppies and hearts across the top. Her hair was pulled back in a ponytail and if she wore any makeup, Liam couldn't see it. She was more beautiful to him than any other woman he could imagine.

That was part of why he hadn't returned to Crimson throughout the years. He liked to think he'd gotten over her but knew he'd never be able to control his physical reaction to her. She could be standing in front of him wearing a potato sack and his body would come to life.

When she glanced in his direction, she must have seen something in his eyes because hers darkened in response, faint spots of color appearing on her cheeks.

"You're not using the cane," she said, turning to Ruth with a smile. "How does your hip feel?"

"Like it was getting rusty," the older woman answered. "It's too crowded to bother with the cane in here." She took the cookie from Austin. "And I didn't want to miss my chance at an early dessert."

"Do you want punch?" he asked. "I can pour you a glass."

Ruth shook her head. "I'll stick with just the cookie. But thank you, Austin. I wish all the boys I've known through the years had your good manners." She threw a look at Liam.

"I was too busy getting in trouble to worry about manners," he told her.

"You turned out okay."

"I give you credit for that," he said honestly.

"Always so sweet," she whispered and dabbed at the corner of her eye. "Liam's going to stay in town for the holidays. Isn't that wonderful?"

"Wonderful," Natalie repeated, her voice sounding dazed. "You can take that much time off work?"

"I'll work from here." He took a glass of punch from the table, wishing he didn't care that his old girlfriend wasn't excited for him to remain close.

"You used to love Christmas," Ruth said, patting his arm. "This will be perfect. There are so many activities around here over the holidays."

"I get two weeks off school," Austin announced.

"Maybe we can all do some fun stuff together when Mom isn't working. You guys used to hang out a lot, right?"

He saw Natalie take a small step back, almost as if she'd been punched in the gut. He knew the feeling. "Sounds great, buddy. I'm looking forward to seeing old friends in town." He turned to Ruth. "In fact, Jason Crenshaw wants to go snowmobiling up on the mountain this weekend if we get that new snow they're predicting. Do you still have helmets at the farm?"

"I do."

Austin jumped up and down in front of him. "Can I come? I've always wanted to try snowmobiling. Some of my friends at school go with their dads."

"Sure," Liam answered automatically. Natalie gave a sharp shake of her head behind Austin. "I mean," he amended, "if it's okay with your mom."

The boy whirled around. "It's okay, Mom. Josh said we could go sometime out on Crimson Ranch when they weren't busy. Now Liam can take me."

Natalie crossed her arms over her chest. Her friends, Josh and Sara Travers, owned the guest ranch outside of town. While she trusted them to keep her precious boy safe, Crimson Ranch was popular enough that Josh would be hard-pressed to find the free time to take her son snowmobiling. That had definitely made it easier to say yes to Austin in the first place. "I don't know. It's pretty dangerous."

"Liam and Mr. Crenshaw will make sure I'm okay."

"You could come, too." Liam snapped shut his mouth, but the words were already out. What the hell possessed him to make that offer? He'd been looking forward to letting off some steam on the mountain with his buddy. Not hosting a pseudo-family outing.

"I don't want to leave Ruth for so long,"

"Of course you should go," Ruth argued. "I can have one of the nurses from the home-care agency fill in if I need it. Besides, I'm feeling much better."

"Please, Mom."

The teacher from Austin's class called the kids to gather at the door. Austin tugged on Natalie's arm. "Ple-eease."

"Fine." Natalie blew out a breath. "We'll both go."

"Yes! You're the best mom ever." Austin threw his arms around Natalie, then hurried off to line up with his class.

"It's fine," Liam said when Natalie shot him a glare.

"Didn't you total the snowmobile Jase's dad owned back in high school?"

"I'm going to walk with Harold back to his room," Ruth said quickly, waving to the older man as she hobbled away.

"I can't believe she ditched me," Liam muttered, then offered Natalie a tentative smile. "I was young and stupid then."

"Now you're older." Natalie continued to stare at him, arms crossed, the toe of her purple clog tapping on the floor.

"And smarter."

"I don't want anything to happen to Austin," she said after a moment. "He's all I've got."

She didn't meet his gaze as she said the words, but he could see how much they cost her. He felt a rush of emotion and a spark of envy. It was irrational and unfair, but Liam didn't have anything—anyone—so precious to him in his life. He hadn't since he'd left Crimson.

"I'll keep him safe, Natalie." He couldn't stop himself from touching her, just a finger on the delicate bone at her wrist. "I'll keep both of you safe."

She went still as his finger grazed her skin. "I'm overreacting," she said after a moment, shifting away from his touch. "It will be fun. Thank you for including us." The words were as stiff as her body language, but Liam didn't press her on it. He wasn't sure what, if anything, he wanted from Natalie again—but had an entire holiday season to figure it out.

Chapter Five

"Are you sure you don't want a beer or a glass of wine?"

"Mom, it's not even five o'clock."

Her mother sat the cup of coffee Natalie had requested on the shiny bar. "It's five o'clock somewhere," she sang in her gravelly alto. "Besides, Lou isn't here so I can give you a drink on the house. One of the perks of the job."

Natalie was pretty sure Lou Bristol, the owner of Crimson's local bar, The Tavern, would comp her a drink if he were there. Natalie's mother, Trudy, had worked for Lou since Natalie was a girl. She'd spent hours in the corner of the bar, playing on the same pinball machine that currently fascinated Austin.

"Have you finished your homework?" she called to her son. The bar was empty save for a couple of regulars who were used to seeing her stop by to visit her mom. It was easier to spend a few minutes with Trudy here than to get stuck in her mother's cramped apartment for an entire evening.

"Yep," Austin answered, shoving a handful of popcorn into his mouth before shooting the pinball once more.

"You're too hard on him," Trudy said as she stacked glasses. "I never hassled you about homework."

You never paid enough attention to realize I had homework, Natalie wanted to answer, but took a long drink of the bitter coffee instead. Normally she wouldn't have caffeine so late in the afternoon, but she was behind on making jewelry for the art fair that was part of the town's big Winterfest event. It was going to be a late night.

"Austin had his school concert at the senior center today." She reached out to straighten a pile of cardboard coasters at the edge of the bar. "They're going to do an evening performance right before school lets out for winter break if you want to come."

Her mother shrugged. "Maybe. I'm taking on extra shifts so some of the girls can have time off for the holidays. I can use the money right before Christmas." She dangled her arm in front of Natalie, wiggling her fingers. "Check out these new rings I got from one of those home shopping channels. They were a great deal. Three easy payments. Real gold, too."

"Nice, Mom." Natalie pushed away her cup, the coffee suddenly burning her stomach. She couldn't remember the last time her mother had been to one of Austin's school or sporting events. Why did she even bother to ask?

"Speaking of money, I hear Liam Donovan's creeping around town again."

Natalie rolled her eyes. "He's not exactly 'creeping.' He came to visit Ruth and I guess he's looking at Crimson for his new company."

"All smoke and mirrors," Trudy said with a sniff. "That boy is trouble. Always has been."

"He hasn't been a boy for a while now, Mom. He's a successful businessman."

Trudy's kohl-rimmed eyes narrowed and Natalie knew she should shut her mouth. Defending Liam to her mother was an old habit, but it only ever served to make Trudy more suspicious. "He should stick to Aspen or Vail or some other ritzy-titzy town. Crimson doesn't need his type."

"The town council might disagree." Natalie hopped off her bar stool.

"Just so long as you stay away from him."

"I've barely got time to brush my teeth, Mom. Dating isn't on my list of priorities."

"Sweetie, you work too hard." Her mom reached across the bar and took Natalie's hand in hers. "I worry about you on your own. Just you and Austin."

"We do all right."

"All right isn't good enough for my daughter and grandson."

Natalie's heart clenched at this kernel of motherly concern, then went hard when her mother added, "I talked to Brad the other day."

"Don't start." Natalie's head whipped around to make sure Austin was still occupied with the pinball machine. "And don't mention his name in front of Austin. He shouldn't hope his deadbeat dad is going come back into his life."

"Don't call your husband a deadbeat, Natalie. How does that reflect on you?"

Natalie tugged her hand away from her mother's. "He's my ex-husband, so he doesn't reflect on me any longer."

"He wants to be a part of your life again. He sounded real sorry for what happened between the two of you. He's sad and lonely, Nat. He needs support—"

"Did he happen to mention that I'm already supporting him, Mom?" Natalie pressed her palms to the cool wood of the bar and leaned forward, pitching her voice low so only Trudy could hear. "Did he tell you that I've not only been paying off the debts he left me, but also giving him money for his current gambling debt? That every time he calls with a sob story about how much he misses his son, what he means is 'give me money or I'll mess up your life again, Nat.'"

"You don't know—"

"I do know." Natalie practically spit the words. "I know that I haven't had a true day off in years. That I worry every night about whether I'll be able to keep the ugly truth about the kind of person his father is from Austin. Do you think I don't know my son needs a father? But not the kind who's willing to gamble away our house and savings, then walk out on us. That's not what either of us needs."

"People make mistakes," Trudy insisted. "If you don't give someone a second chance—"

"They won't have an opportunity to screw you over again." Natalie shook her head. "I'm not taking Brad back, Mom. Now or ever."

Trudy pursed her lips but didn't say anything more. She didn't need to. Her mother had a blind spot where Brad was concerned. As much as Trudy hated Liam Donovan, she loved Brad Holt. Her mom had been Brad's biggest champion since Natalie first dated him, and she wondered how much she'd allowed her mother's opinion to color her own.

Maybe she would have seen Brad's true colors early enough to change course if her relationship with him hadn't given her a strange bond with her mother. It was a connection she'd always craved but never been able to sustain on her own. But even if she still wanted more from her mom, letting her ex-husband back into her life was not an option.

She called Austin over to say goodbye to his grandma, then bundled them both up and headed out of the bar. It was still afternoon, but already the light was fading. Lights twinkled up and down Crimson's main street, with the shops cheerfully decorated for the holidays. Tourism was a big piece of the town's economy. Crimson benefited from its proximity to Aspen and was also gaining a reputation as a mountain destination in its own right thanks to the hard work of the community.

"I smell snow," Austin said as they walked to where Natalie had parked on a side street.

She smiled. "Me, too, buddy."

"Maybe I'll have a day off tomorrow."

"We'll see." Natalie knew how much kids looked forward to snow days, but she had a morning shift at the senior center so secretly crossed her fingers that school wouldn't be canceled.

"Snow day, snow day," Austin chanted, raising his fists in the air.

"Be sure to sleep with a spoon under your pillow," a voice called from nearby.

"Good idea, Mr. Crenshaw."

Jason Crenshaw came to stand in front of the two of them. "Remember, you can call me Jase. We're friends, I hope."

"I'm going snowmobiling with you and Liam on Saturday," Austin answered.

"We'll have a great time." He looked at Natalie. "Can I talk to you for a second?"

"Sure." She hit a button on her key fob to unlock the door. "Austin, hop in. I'll be right there."

She turned to Jase as the car door shut. "What's up?" Natalie had known Jason Crenshaw most of her life. They'd actually been neighbors growing up in an apartment complex near the edge of town that housed mostly blue-collar families and ski resort workers who couldn't afford to live in Aspen.

Jase had been a skinny, nerdy kid but had grown into his looks and body in recent years, with the easy grace of a man totally comfortable with who he was. But he didn't look so comfortable now.

"Are you still thinking of running for mayor next year?" she asked, stuffing her hands in her pockets to ward off the cold.

He nodded. "That's actually part of why I need to talk to you. I hate to even bring this up, Natalie, but—"

Her stomach hit the ground. Jase had been her divorce attorney and was still trying to help her get rid of Brad for good. He was one of the few people who knew the whole truth of what she was facing. "It's okay, Jase. I should have the rest of your payment by the end of the month. I've been trying to save a little extra for Christmas and—"

"It's not about the money," he said quickly. "It's about Liam."

Natalie swallowed. "Liam?"

"You've heard he's considering Crimson as a headquarters for his new company?"

"I think everyone between here and Grand Junction has heard that rumor."

"It's a big deal for the town, and we're going to pull out all the stops to make the deal go through." He adjusted the wire-rimmed glasses he wore, not making eye contact with her. "I'd appreciate any help you could give on that front."

"I don't have much influence with town council, Jase."

"I mean with Liam."

"Oh." Now it was her turn to avoid eye contact. "I'm not sure I have any influence with Liam."

"You used to."

"A long time ago," she said softly. "You know how that ended."

Jase nodded, looking as if he wanted the sidewalk to swallow him whole. "I'm sorry, Nat. I shouldn't have said anything. I'd never take advantage of our friendship or put you in a bad situation. It's just that I don't want Liam's old feelings about Crimson to color his decision about the future."

"It's okay." Natalie took her hand out of her pocket to pat his arm. "You've helped me out of a lot of bad situations. I owe you, way more than money."

"You don't," Jase told her. "Again, I'm sorry. There are so many things I want to see happen in this town, but it's hard to convince some of the old guard that change can be good. LifeMap coming here could help get the ball rolling. But I don't want to make you uncomfortable."

"If it comes up, I'll encourage Liam," Natalie offered. She really did owe Jase a lot. "Not that he cares about my opinion, but I'll try."

Jase let out a huge breath, his hazel eyes shining behind his glasses. "Thanks, Natalie. That would be a huge help." He wrapped her in a quick hug. "I hope Liam can put the past behind him. And we're going to take care of your more recent past, too. We'll find a way to get Brad out of your life for good."

"Thank you," she whispered, disconcerted to hear Liam's name brought up along with her ex-husband's. Two of her biggest mistakes in life. No, that wasn't exactly true. Her marriage to Brad had been a mistake.

Liam was simply a regret. Regret that she hadn't been enough to hold him and in some deep, secret place that she'd let him walk away so easily.

Liam eased his SUV down the driveway of Ruth's small farm Saturday morning. Nerves skittered through his stomach and he shook his head. With all he'd accomplished in his life, why did taking his ex-girlfriend and her son snowmobiling make him edgy?

Natalie had always had that effect on him, from the moment he'd caught sight of her in the hall his first day at the local high school. Even then, she'd been totally self-contained, sure of herself and who she was. Natalie never seemed to need anyone, which had made Liam want her all the more. He'd wanted to break down her walls and know the person behind the tough-girl mask she always wore.

For a while he thought he had. He'd thought their connection, their love, would be one for the ages, would fill up all the misaligned pieces in his own heart. But like most everyone else he'd let himself love, she'd rejected him. Liam had been a master of disappointing the people around him, then pushing them away.

That was old news. He'd moved on, made a success of his life and had returned to Crimson able to hold his head high. He wasn't the rich-boy goof-off so many people had thought. Now the town was courting him. Whether he ended up moving his company here didn't even matter, not to him. What counted was that finally he was wanted in this small corner of the world.

He knew the moment Natalie realized that it was him and not Jase picking up her and Austin for the day. Her body went rigid. Even under her thick parka and ski pants he could see the tension. Austin waved and threw a handful of snow into the air. The kid's innocent excitement made Liam smile, despite Natalie's obvious reaction.

He lowered the window on the passenger side as he pulled to a stop in front of them. "Are you two ready to go?"

"I can't wait." Austin opened the back door and jumped into the car. "How fast do the snowmobiles go? Can I drive? We won't roll over, right?"

Liam tipped his head to the backseat. "As fast as your mom thinks is safe. No, you can't drive, and no one is going to roll today."

Natalie came closer but didn't open the door. "Where's Jase? I thought he was picking us up and we were meeting you at the trailhead."

"He called his morning," Liam answered. He threw the car into Park and walked around the front of it to where she stood. "Some last-minute deposition he had to take for a trial that starts next week."

Her eyes narrowed and he raised his palms. "I swear, Nat. Do you want to call him?"

"I believe you," she muttered under her breath. "I'm not so sure about Jase's story. Maybe we should reschedule for a time he can go, too."

"Do you think he's trying to push us together?" He felt a smile curve the corner of his mouth. "Like he's setting us up or something."

She shook her head. "No. I don't know. It doesn't matter. Nothing is going to happen between us."

"Right," Liam agreed although the hammering of his heart as he looked at her told a different story. He tried, once again, to ignore his body's reaction to her. Today she wore a dark purple parka and a fleece cap. As forecasted, it had snowed overnight, and she looked especially bright and beautiful against the backdrop of the crisp white mountain shadowing the farm. "If you want to cancel today, you're going to have one disappointed kid on your hands."

Her eyes flicked to Austin in the backseat.

"Come on, Mom. Get in," her son called.

"He's so excited."

"It'll be fun, Nat. I promise."

She bit down on her lip as if considering her options, and Liam held his breath.

"Fine. Fun," she said after a moment.

Trying not to look relieved, he opened the SUV's door for her, then climbed back in and started the drive up Crimson Mountain.

Chapter Six

Natalie's stomach dipped and swayed as Liam drove the winding road up the mountain. Although snow blanketed the valley below and the branches of the pine trees in the surrounding forest, the road was clear and dry for most of the ride. The snowplow drivers were out early in Crimson, and she was used to winter driving.

Her butterflies had more to do with the man sitting next to her, his arm resting casually on the console between them. His olive-colored down jacket made his eyes look more intense than normal. To Natalie, Liam had always been the perfect combination of rugged good looks and polished sophistication that came from his fancy upbringing. Not much had changed in ten years.

He turned onto one of the forest service roads, and a sign announced they'd be at the River Run Sports Park in two miles. It was a slow drive. Natalie tried to keep her attention focused on the scenery and not Liam's strong fingers gripping the steering wheel. Even so, she felt her skin grow warm as he absently rubbed the back of his neck.

He flashed a grin as she adjusted the temperature on her side of the SUV. "Too warm?" he asked.

"Just fine," she answered and tucked her hands under her legs on the leather seat.

Austin chattered from the backseat, peppering Liam with detailed questions about the machines he'd rented. Her son had an engineer's brain from the time he said his first words, and she was surprised Liam could answer the nine-year-old's array of questions easily and with so much patience.

The mountain sports outfitter's cabin came into view a few minutes later. Liam parked and Austin bolted from the car to where two shiny snowmobiles were parked nearby. A burly man came out of the building to greet them. "I've got your machines all ready, Mr. Donovan."

"Thanks," Liam said, looking almost embarrassed at the deference the older man showed him. "Call me Liam. I appreciate you taking care of everything."

"You bet." The man stuck out his hand and Liam shook it. "I'm Mark Wright, the owner here. I…uh…have been thinking of expanding the operation. If you like what you see today, maybe we can talk about an investment?"

She saw Liam close his eyes for a moment and take a deep breath before answering. "Maybe. Either way, we're looking forward to a day on the mountain."

"It's a perfect one," Mark agreed. He glanced at Natalie then back at Liam. "I thought Jase was coming out with you."

"He had to cancel. It's just the three of us."

Mark raised his bushy brows at Natalie. "You know how to drive one of these things, honey?"

Natalie's nerves turned to temper in an instant. The

guy was fawning all over Liam but barely made eye contact with her. "I'm not your 'honey' and I grew up in Crimson. I can handle a snowmobile." She hoped that was the case, since she technically hadn't been on one in years. She figured it must be like riding a bike.

"Feisty," Mark said with a nod in Liam's direction. "I like it."

Natalie felt her mouth drop open. She narrowed her eyes at Liam.

"Me, too," he said to Mark, and she could tell it was a struggle for him to keep a straight face.

"Which one of you is taking the boy?" Mark led them over to the snowmobiles.

"Can I ride with you, Liam?" Austin asked, running his gloved hand along the side of the machine. "I know you'll go faster than Mom."

"You don't know anything of the sort," Natalie said with a huff.

"That's true," Liam agreed. "Your mother had quite the lead foot back in the day. How many speeding tickets did you get senior year, Nat?"

She made a slicing gesture across her throat as Austin turned to her, his eyes wide with something that strangely looked like newfound respect. "You used to drive fast, Mom?" He grinned at her. "That's kind of cool."

"It was a long time ago." Natalie adjusted Austin's fleece hat with its camo pattern. It seemed like not that long ago his favorite winter hat had Cookie Monster's face on it. Time went by so quickly.

"Can I ride with Liam?"

She nodded. "If that's okay with him."

"Does everyone have helmets?" Mark asked.

Natalie started to shake her head, but Liam nodded. "Let me grab them from the car."

He was back a moment later, handing Natalie a deep maroon helmet and Austin one in hunter green. "These aren't from Ruth's," she said as she put it on.

"I had my assistant pick them up in Aspen. No big deal."

No big deal except the cost of the helmets and the price of renting snowmobiles for the day were luxuries Natalie could never afford on her own. There was so much she wanted to give her son that she couldn't until she was financially stable. That seemed like a goal always just out of reach.

"Ready?" Liam asked softly, pulling her from her unwelcome thoughts. His eyes were too gentle as he looked at her. She flipped on her goggles and nodded.

Mark gave them instructions on the course. She climbed onto one of the machines and started the engine the way he showed her.

"Hold on tight," she heard Liam yell, and Austin grabbed on to him as if he trusted Liam implicitly. How she wished life was so simple for her.

They took off toward the single track snaking into the forest. As she followed, all her worries and concerns melted away, drowned out by the loud hum of the snowmobile's engine and the beauty of the pristine landscape.

The trail was clearly marked and well groomed, but Natalie felt as if they'd entered a different world. Snow weighted the branches of the trees, forming a canopy over the trail. Sunlight filtered through, making patterns of light and shadow on all the white that surrounded them. It would have been peaceful other than the roar and vibration of the engine filling the otherwise quiet air. Adrenaline rushed through her as they zipped farther up the mountain. She relaxed as the mechanics of handling a snowmobile came back to her. She held back, then raced forward, testing her control of the machine.

Liam held a steady speed and slowed on turns, which she knew was for her benefit. Occasionally their movements would loosen a chunk of snow from above and she'd be showered in sparkling crystal flakes. It was a dry snow at this time of year, light and fluffy—it felt as if she'd been dropped into a picture postcard.

She trusted that Liam knew where he was going, trusted him more than she'd thought she would with Austin. As they entered a wide-open meadow he slowed, allowing her to come up next to him and giving her a thumbs-up sign as question. She glanced at Austin, gave a thumbs-up signal in return then gunned her engine, shooting off across the field of pristine snow. She loved the speed and the thrill of finally being able to outrun the stress of real life. Although she'd been reluctant to come on this outing, she realized how much both she and her son needed this day of fun.

After almost an hour they came to a stop at the top of a rise. Natalie turned off her machine and loosened the helmet and goggles she wore.

"Mom, that was awesome," Austin yelled, his voice echoing in the sudden silence of the clearing.

"It sure was," she agreed, realizing she was smiling as broadly as her son.

Liam pointed to a wooden table and bench that sat at the edge of hill, a path to them shoveled and lined with stones. "Anyone for a hot chocolate break?" He climbed off and took off a pack that had been strapped to the back of the machine.

"Me!" Austin scrambled off the snowmobile. "Are there snacks, too?"

"Chocolate-chip cookies from the bakery in town."

"Katie's cookies?" Austin took the pack Liam handed him. "This is the best day ever. Right, Mom?"

"You bet, buddy." Her gaze crashed into Liam's. "The best," she whispered. And the fact that the best day she could remember in forever involved Liam rocked her to her core.

"You can drop us at home. This is too much."

"Mom, he's got a *hot tub*." Austin put special emphasis on the two words, as if the Holy Grail was waiting behind Liam's front door.

Liam pulled into the oversize garage at his house. He wasn't sure why he'd offered pizza and the hot tub after they'd finished snowmobiling. Scratch that. He knew exactly why. Because he didn't want the day to end. He wanted to keep Natalie with him as long as possible, clearly a glutton for punishment.

As much fun as he'd had snowmobiling, it hadn't been enough. Besides, something had happened when they'd stopped for hot chocolate. Natalie had taken off her helmet and for a moment he'd seen a glimpse of the girl he remembered, her smile brighter than the Colorado sun shining in the bluebird sky. It wasn't the motherly and nurturing smile she gave to Austin or the compassionate one he'd seen her flash to the residents at the senior center.

It had been full of so much pure joy, it had changed her. Shaken off the past decade, making her appear vibrant and alive in a way he wished he could bottle. She'd never been one for huge displays of emotion, which made the ones she did reveal so much better. The fact that something he'd arranged put that smile on her face made him feel as though he was the luckiest guy on the planet.

Yet when she'd admitted that she was having a good time, the smile slipped and her walls had gone up again. The ones he didn't quite understand. She was probably smart to keep a distance between them, but he still didn't like it. There was so much of Natalie's life that he wasn't a part of. It was none of his business. But it didn't stop him from wanting to know more.

"You don't have to stay late," he told her as they climbed out of the car.

"It's the weekend, Mom." Austin tugged on her arm as she held back. Liam opened the door to the house and they followed him through. "And Ms. Ruth and the other nurse are watching a movie. Live a little."

He walked past them both into the kitchen.

"Did my kid just tell me to 'live a little'?"

"I'm sure he meant it in the most respectful way possible."

"I'm sure," she agreed sarcastically.

"This kitchen is huge," Austin said as he circled around the large room. "You stay here by yourself?"

For a moment, Liam saw the space through the boy's eyes. The vaulted ceilings and enormous six-burner stove with the custom stainless range hood over it. The counters were polished marble and the floors a creamy travertine tile that contrasted with the rich cherry cabinets. It had been so long since Liam had even registered the places where he stayed when he traveled. Tanner booked everything, and his assistant's taste was much finer than Liam's.

Now he wished he paid more attention to the house he'd rented outside of Crimson. It felt almost gaudy in comparison to the homeyness of the farmhouse. As if he was lording his wealth, which may have been his intention but seemed crass now that he saw how little Natalie and Austin had in their lives.

He met Natalie's gaze, took in the thin line of her mouth. "My assistant is here, too," he offered, realizing he sounded lame. "He rented the place. I didn't realize how big it was until I got here."

She crooked a brow and he took off his cap, tossing it on the counter and rubbing one hand through his hair. "I just meant it wasn't exactly my idea."

"Is he blaming this monstrosity on me?" Tanner walked into the room, his attention focused on Austin. Liam stepped behind Natalie, waving his arms and shaking his head, trying to stop the overshare of information he knew was coming next. "My instructions were to find the biggest house on the mountain. He was going to show…" Tanner broke off as he turned to see Natalie. "To show his…uh…nanny that…um…all that time getting him to do his homework had paid off. That he was a success."

"The lesson," Liam said quickly, moving in front of Natalie, "is that if you do your homework, good things will happen."

Tanner nodded, and Liam decided he might not kill the other man tonight.

Austin looked between the two of them as if they were crazy. Liam felt crazy until Natalie laughed. Just a small sound, but it loosened the coils around his heart. Even if she was laughing *at* him, he'd take it.

"I'm Natalie Holt," she said, reaching out a hand to Tanner. "Ruth's nurse."

"I know who you are, darlin'." Tanner took her hand, lifting it to his lips.

"Too thick," Liam mumbled. "Laying it on too thick."

But Natalie laughed again. "The house is lovely. We're happy to be here."

"You are?" Liam asked.

Tanner shook his head. "Always the smooth operator with the ladies."

"Shut it, Tanner."

His assistant only smirked. "A couple quick real-life things to mention. One of the investors needs to move up the meeting to next week. You have about twenty messages waiting from some of the other guys who'd planned to be there."

"Work it out," he said.

"Will do," Tanner said with a nod. "The new tech guy fixed the bug with the app. It should be able to sync with no connection issues now."

Liam felt then saw Natalie take a step away. "You're obviously busy here. We don't need to take up any more of your time."

"Mom," Austin whined.

"It's okay." Liam threw a look to Tanner. "There's nothing that needs my immediate attention, right?"

"Right," the other man agreed, seeming somewhat shocked. Liam didn't blame him. He was kind of a micromanager, wanting to know every detail that involved his business. It might be part of the reason he'd been so successful, but now he realized it was mostly a result of not caring about anything else in his life.

"I'm off the clock tonight," he said.

Tanner grinned in response. "It's about damn time. Let's get this party started." He turned to the boy. "You must be Austin."

"How do you know my name?"

"Liam pays me to know everything. I'm guessing that swimsuit you're holding is for the hot tub?"

"We ordered pizza, too," Austin told him.

"Extra cheese?"

"And pepperoni," Austin confirmed. "But no veggies."

"A boy after my own heart. Come with me and I'll show you where to get changed."

Austin glanced at Natalie who nodded. "We'll meet you there, bud."

"You're getting in, too. Right, Mom? You brought your swimsuit." Austin pointed to the bag she had slung over her shoulder.

"Sure," she whispered as color flooded her cheeks.

"A hot tub party," Tanner said with a grin. "I love it. About time Liam got a decent social life."

Liam rolled his eyes as Tanner left the room with the boy. Maybe he wouldn't kill him, but could he get away with firing him?

He turned to Natalie. "Do you want a glass of water or a beer or wine first?" *Or a cold shower*? Because the thought of seeing her in a bathing suit after all these years made him want to dive headfirst in a snowbank to regain control.

"I'm fine," she said, gripping her bag as if it was a life raft on the *Titanic*. "I should...go with Tanner and Austin." Before he could answer, she hurried from the room.

He started to follow, then turned and strode to the refrigerator, yanking open the freezer door and grabbing an ice pack. He pressed it to his forehead, flinching against the cold at the same time he welcomed the sting of it. Cooling off. That's what Liam needed right now. A good cooling off.

Chapter Seven

No big deal.

I don't care what Liam Donovan thinks.

She stood in front of the large mirror in the guest bathroom where Tanner had led her to change. It was only a powder room, a half bath near the rear of the house but it was bigger than any bathroom Natalie had seen in her life. And, unfortunately, better lit.

Opening one eye, she glanced at herself and quickly turned away. The bathing suit she wore was modest, a tankini top and board shorts. She'd bought it several years ago when she was more concerned with being able to splash in the community pool with Austin than impress a guy. There was nothing impressive about this swimsuit. Only a bit of her belly and back showed between below the tankini's hem, but it was enough to expose the faded crescents from the stretch marks she'd gotten during her pregnancy. Liam may have known her body once upon a time, but she wasn't a teenager anymore and knew she was no competition for the women normally a part of his world.

Then she sucked in a breath and gave herself a mental headshake. Her body was strong and reliable. The only reason she was in a bathing suit right now was to make her son happy. She wished she could give Austin a day like this every weekend. If he wanted her in the hot tub, that's where she'd be.

When she walked out onto the patio, she crossed her arms over her chest against the cold. It was a clear evening, the sun already dipping behind the mountain as darkness enveloped the property around the house. Darkness was good if she was going to be hanging out in her bathing suit. The sound of bubbling water and her son's laughter drew her to the far corner to the patio.

"Hey, Mom," Austin called when he spotted her. "You've got to try this seat. The jets spray all over your back."

She paused as she caught sight of Liam, who was perched on the edge, his feet dangling in the water. The goose bumps that erupted on her skin suddenly had nothing to do with the cold air. They were because of him. All for him.

He was broader now, more defined, more of a man. The hard planes and angles of his arms and chest made her breath lodge in her throat. He was totally masculine yet unaware of how perfect he was. She wondered if he'd honed his body at an expensive gym or with the extracurricular activities—deep-sea diving, rock climbing, skiing—that rich people seemed to gravitate toward.

She wanted to run, to hide her own body, very much in need of a workout beyond lifting seniors in and out of bed. He swallowed as his gaze tangled with hers, as if he couldn't quite catch his breath, either. That gave her a little more confidence, enough to keep her feet moving.

"Mom, aren't you cold?" Austin asked, breaking the spell between her and Liam.

"Scoot over, bud," Liam said, clearing his throat. "Give her some room."

Keeping her eyes on where she was going—no need to tumble headfirst into the hot tub—she placed one foot then the other into the water. It was hot, so hot it almost stung, but that didn't stop her from sinking into the corner seat as quickly as she could. Her body shivered from the change in temperature.

"I'll fix the sprays," Austin said, oblivious to the tension that seemed to crackle in the air between her and Liam. She couldn't help but relax a little as the water jetted into the muscles of her back, working against the knots she carried. "This is even better than the hot springs. Right, Mom?"

"It's pretty good," she agreed, tucking a stray hair behind her ear. Steam rose around her and she sank lower until the water almost touched her chin.

"Do you mean the hot springs over in Grand Junction?" Liam asked.

Austin nodded. "Mom and I went for a weekend when I was like seven. There's a really good fudge place in town, too."

"Where's the best place you've been on vacation?"

"Um…" Her eyes tracked to her son as he thought about the question. "Maybe Colorado Springs," he offered after a moment. "I thought Garden of the Gods was cool and they've got this North Pole place with rides. Everyone dresses like elves and Christmas music always plays. Back when I believed in Santa Claus, that's where I thought he lived."

"Don't let Ms. Ruth hear you say you don't believe in Santa." Liam bent forward to splash his arms, making them shine as the water dripped off again. "One year she banned me from Christmas cookies for the whole season because I told one of the girls at school there was no Santa."

"That's harsh," Austin agreed.

"So Colorado Springs?" Liam asked, and Natalie felt her already warm face flush even hotter.

Austin nodded. "We don't travel too many places. Mom's afraid to fly—"

"I remember that."

"And she can't get much time off work so it's hard to go on a road trip."

"We might try Moab over spring break," she offered quickly, shame bubbling like the tiny pockets of air she popped at the water's surface.

"Moab would be cool."

She couldn't meet her son's gaze right now, or Liam's. She realized she'd done to Austin exactly what she'd resented her mother for, for so much of her youth. She'd insulated him, walled him off in this small town because of her fear. Her fear of losing control, of losing him to the big bad world outside of Crimson. But bad things could happen right here. She knew that better than most.

She glanced up through her moist eyelashes to see Liam watching her. He knew. Her dirty little secret, her overwhelming fear. He could see past her excuses of money and time to where the truth was buried deep inside her. She'd hated her mother's constant stream of ranting about how things were so different and dangerous outside of Crimson.

Yet that belief had seeped into Natalie's pores, become part of her DNA and had colored every choice she'd made in life. There was no use denying it, and as much as she wanted to, it made her almost physically ill to think that someday Austin would yearn for more and he'd leave her behind in her sad, lonely, box of a life.

"Pizza's here." Tanner's deep voice cut through her internal self-flagellation.

She swiped the tips of her fingers under her eyes, hoping the sheen of moisture on her cheeks disguised the errant tears that escaped. Her life didn't leave time for tears.

She turned a bright smile on her son. "I bet you're hungry after today."

"Starving," Austin agreed, standing and shaking the water from his hair like a puppy.

Liam's oversize assistant stepped forward, placing a pile of fluffy towels on the wrought-iron table nearby, then handing one to Austin as he jumped out of the hot tub.

"We'll be right there," Liam told Tanner. Out of the corner of her eye, she saw the assistant nod and lead Austin away, telling him about the Xbox in the rec room downstairs.

"It's like he's Willy Wonka," Natalie said after a moment.

"Tanner is a big kid at heart, but he's like my right hand. I couldn't manage without him."

She kept her gaze on the water, but lifted herself out a bit, afraid she might overheat otherwise. "You probably think I'm the worst mom in history."

"Is that a joke?" His gentle tone made her teeth hurt, as if she'd just taken a bite of too-sweet candy.

"He's nine years old and hasn't even been out of the state."

"So what?" Liam hit a button on the control panel and the bubbles stopped, leaving only a soft fizzing sound in their place. "I traveled all over with my parents as a kid. It meant they could spend money, not that they loved me. Ruth never took me any place beyond school, but she was the only adult I ever believed truly cared about me."

"It's not about the money," she said on an angry hiss of breath. "The money is a factor but not the whole story, so don't bother pretending otherwise." She lifted her gaze to his. "You know it's my stupid, irrational fear. I've let it trap me here and if I'm not careful, I'm going to do the same thing to Austin."

She expected him to agree, to rehash how she'd ruined what they'd had with her ridiculous and seemingly insurmountable anxiety about the world beyond her hometown. Each time she tried to convince herself that her fears were unfounded, life tended to rear up and slap her down, tighten the chains that kept her tethered to Crimson.

Instead his eyes were tender. "We both made mistakes, Natalie. I understood your fears and how much worse they got after Beth died. Her death in that car accident damaged more people than just Logan, Jake and Josh. It's horrible that they lost their sister, but it wrecked all of us."

"It wasn't your fault—"

"I let it drive us apart, Nat. I knew your mom was trying to poison you against me and I pushed you too hard, too fast. I closed you and Ruth out because of my own guilt."

She shook her head, unwilling to hear these words from Liam after so long. It was as if he was trying to slip through the cracks in her hard shell, as if she still might have some warmth left at her center.

It wasn't true. There was no room for anything but Austin and her fierce need to keep him safe. From his father, from the pain of not being wanted by one of your parents that Natalie had grown up feeling. She'd made too many mistakes, and she couldn't afford to show Liam or anyone how out of control her life had become. How alone she was, even in this town where she knew so many people by name.

"You don't have to say that, Liam. It doesn't matter anymore."

Another lie. It mattered to her as much as her next breath. As he continued to watch her, the energy between them shifted. The fact that they were alone and mostly undressed registered deep inside her. That pull, the connection that was always between them, gained strength and momentum. Natalie stood abruptly, the cold night air engulfing her, but she didn't feel any cooler.

She scrambled out of the hot tub and grabbed one of the plush towels, her fingers shaking as she wrapped it around her shoulders.

Liam was behind her in an instant, his strong fingers tucking the towel around her, grazing the skin at her collarbone as he did.

"I don't want to be the enemy anymore," he whispered against her ear. "The stupidest thing I ever did was walk away from you. Trust me, I've visited every damn continent and nothing compares to being with you. You were my whole world, and I was an idiot to let you go."

No! her mind screamed, his words wrecking her.

Yes, her heart whispered, finally vindicated in its decadelong yearning for him.

The moment, the emotion of it was too much. She couldn't let him inside again, but her legs wouldn't walk away. She whirled, ready to push and rail and ruin this second chance before he could break her heart again. But the vulnerability, the need in his eyes stopped her. Without thinking or worrying about the consequences, she lifted her face and pressed her mouth to his.

* * *

This kiss rocked Liam. He'd taken a big risk by saying what he did to Natalie. He knew she liked her life ordered and contained, and he'd thought she might run. Instead she kissed him with a fierceness he barely recognized.

She claimed him with that kiss and he welcomed it, his hands pushing aside the towel to press her against his length as their tongues met. She bit at his bottom lip and raked her nails across his back, making him hiss in a combination of pain and pleasure. He ran his fingers over her bathing suit top, molding his hands around her waist. To that small band of skin that had tempted him from the moment she'd stepped into the light of the patio.

He didn't feel the frigid evening air. Every part of him was on fire. He heard her soft gasp when he cupped her bottom, pulling her tighter to the front of him, needing her to know how much he wanted her. He dipped his head to kiss the column of her neck, flipping her bathing suit strap off her shoulder. Moving lower, he licked at the swell of her breast, but just as he would have taken her nipple in his mouth, she jerked away. Bending to scoop the towel that had pooled at her feet, she took several steps toward the house.

"Natalie," he said, his voice hoarse with desire. "This isn't over between us. What we had is nowhere near finished."

She adjusted her strap, then pulled the towel tighter around her shoulders. "I don't know if I can do this again, Liam." Now she met his gaze. "I'm not the same girl I was back then."

He walked toward her slowly, not wanting to frighten her off. She looked as skittish as a stray animal, just waiting to be kicked or shooed away. "I'm not the same, either. I want to know you now. Who you are. Who you've become."

"You can't—"

"I do, Natalie. Give me a chance." He bent, his head level with hers until she looked him in the eye. "Give us another chance. Can you do that?"

She bit down on her lip. "I don't know." She turned, took two more steps toward the house, then looked back at him over her shoulder. "Liam?"

"Yeah?"

"That question you asked the other night. Whether I missed you, if I thought about you?" She gave him a whisper of a smile. "I did. Every single day I did."

Then she disappeared into the house, and a shiver ran through him, his body finally registering the cold.

Chapter Eight

"Pancakes or waffles?" Natalie pulled a jar of flour out of the cabinet next to Ruth's refrigerator.

"Pancakes," Austin answered immediately. He looked up from his Lego pieces to where Ruth sat next to him at the kitchen table. "Is that okay with you, Ms. Ruth?"

Natalie's heart burst with pride at her son's sweetness.

Ruth concentrated on fitting together two blue blocks. "I like pancakes," she said. "Used to make them for little Liam every Saturday morning."

"Little Liam still likes pancakes," a deep voice said from the doorway.

The measuring cup Natalie held in her hand clattered to the counter, flour spilling everywhere. She quickly swept it up with her hand, then dumped the powder into the sink.

"Did you do your chores this morning?" Ruth asked. "And wash your hands?"

Natalie turned, meeting Liam's gaze across the room.

She saw him draw in a breath and wanted to reach out, to offer him some support. With her specialization in geriatric nursing, she was used to the slow mental decline of seniors, how the past often became more real to them than the present.

"Liam can help me with breakfast," she offered. "There's a quart of strawberries to be washed and cut in the refrigerator."

"Great." His relief was palpable and Ruth seemed satisfied, once again occupied with stacking Austin's leftover Lego bricks.

"She usually becomes more lucid as the day goes on," Natalie told him quietly as he stepped close to open the refrigerator. He smelled like cold air and shampoo, the ends of his hair still damp. For a moment he paused, hand on the door and looked down at her, swayed closer for a moment. His gray eyes captured hers, and the memory of his hands on her body washed over her like the heat from a banked fire.

"Did you have a good week?" he asked softly.

"Busy," she whispered. She'd been avoiding him since last weekend, since she'd practically attacked him on his patio. He'd told her he wanted a second chance and her reaction had been to maul him, like some crazy undersexed spinster desperate for any physical contact. Which she might be, but still…she liked to believe she had some pride left.

Onc eyebrow lifted in silent question. It took her a moment to track back to the conversation at hand. Nope, not crazy at all.

"I took on an extra shift at the senior center and I'm trying to get a bunch of jewelry made before Winterfest."

"I've seen posters around town. That's the carnival next weekend?"

She nodded. "They have a craft fair on Saturday afternoon. I wasn't going to participate, but my friend Olivia insisted." She placed her fingers around the refrigerator handle, careful not to touch his hand and opened the door.

He stepped back and she took out a carton of eggs and handed him the strawberries. "How was your week?"

A ghost of a smile played across his lips. "The good people of Crimson are certainly rolling out the red carpet to entice me to bring LifeMap to town."

She cracked an egg into a bowl and added a half cup of buttermilk, whipping the mixture together. Her first instinct was a sarcastic comment about how much more at home he'd feel in the flashier Aspen. She stopped herself, remembering her conversation with Jase, thinking of what she owed her old friend.

"Crimson is a vibrant community," she answered instead. "A lot of younger people and families are moving into town. It's changing the dynamic. The area has a lot to offer."

"Does the town council have you on retainer?"

He gave a small laugh as she handed him a cutting board and pointed to the block of knives across the counter. "I've been here my whole life. Who better to promote Crimson's finer points?"

"I remember when you were determined to leave this place."

"It was more my determination to stay with you," she said before she thought about her answer. That was what lack of sleep would do, produce unnecessary honesty. She adjusted the burner on the stove and dropped a pat of butter onto the pan warming there. "What about you? Are you really thinking of returning to Crimson for the long haul or is this just some game you're playing?"

His hand stilled as he dumped the sliced strawberries into the bowl but he didn't look at her. "Game?"

"I know how angry you were when you left here. You felt like people in town blamed you for—"

"I was an outsider. Of course they blamed me." He took a mug from the cabinet and poured a cup of coffee. "I certainly blamed myself."

"You weren't driving."

"I was—"

"Mom, can we have chocolate chips in the pancakes?"

She glanced to the kitchen table. "Sure thing, buddy." Ruth's eyes were knowing. Sometimes the woman was lost in the past and other times as perceptive as ever.

"Liam, we're decorating and hanging ornaments tonight," Ruth called. "You should come over to help."

"Do you still have the singing Santa Claus?" he asked, placing his coffee mug on the counter and pulling out a chair next to Ruth at the table.

"Of course I do," the older woman said with a smile. "Stan and I used to shop the after-Christmas sales—we got the best deals on our decorations that way."

He took her hands in his, kissing the swollen knuckles and Natalie's heart gave an extra fast thump.

His love for Ruth was clear on his face, but he'd stayed away from Crimson for so many years because of what had happened in the past. She knew his relationship with his parents had never been close and it made her sad to think that he'd been missing out on any unconditional warmth in his life. It was stupid, she knew. Liam probably had more friends and possibly lovers than she could count. But something about him in this small farmhouse made her believe that this meant more.

"Is it okay if Tanner comes, too?" he asked, his gaze swinging between Ruth and Natalie. "He's a sucker for the holidays."

"Of course," Ruth answered. "Any of your friends are

welcome here. If you want to invite some guys from the football team, there's plenty of room."

"Tanner works for me, Ruth," Liam said gently. "My football days are over, but thank you for offering that. How about we bring dinner?"

"And brownies from the bakery?" Austin prompted.

"You haven't even had breakfast," Natalie said with a smile. "And already you're planning dessert?"

"You love Katie's brownies more than anyone," her son retorted.

"Brownies sound delicious." Ruth sat up, rubbing her stomach. "I'm hungry."

Natalie laughed. "I'd better get breakfast going quick before I have a mutiny on my hands."

Liam began to help Austin put together the Lego set, reading the instructions and listening intently as her son explained the differences in Lego ninja warriors. Her heart responded to that even more. As much as she tried to be everything for her son—to throw balls, get excited about bugs, listen to endless details about fast cars and big machines—there was no way for her to replace the lack of a father in his life. She understood that loss better than most.

She dropped scoops of batter onto the hot skillet, then added a sprinkling of chips to each one. As they cooked, she poured juice and took out plates and forks, trying to keep herself busy so she wasn't tempted to watch Liam and Austin together, to imagine what could have been if she hadn't pushed Liam away all those years ago.

The bells over the bakery door jingled as Liam walked through. He could have sent Tanner on this errand, but he hadn't mentioned the brownie promise to his assistant.

For some reason it seemed important that he be the one to personally handle dinner and dessert tonight. Besides, Tanner was busy arranging the other supplies.

A cute woman behind the counter straightened, waving him forward as she set a tray on top of the display cabinet. "Welcome to Life is Sweet," she said, transferring cookies to a large platter. After a moment she glanced up. "How can I…" Her voice trailed off as she caught sight of him. Her eyes narrowed and Liam searched his brain for a name. She looked vaguely familiar, with dark brown shoulder-length hair and a heart-shaped face, but he couldn't quite place her.

"I'm Katie Garrity," she said, as if reading his mind. "I was a year behind you at the high school." She paused then added, "I'm friends with Natalie."

He gave her a quick nod at the same time he cursed himself for not having Tanner pick up the damn brownies. "It's nice to meet—or remeet—you." He stuck out his hand and she shook it, looking almost surprised he'd offered it. "I'm actually here to pick up brownies for Natalie and her son. We're hanging Christmas ornaments at my nan—at Ruth's house tonight."

Katie's face relaxed a little. "I have a fresh batch cooling in the back—the ones with a caramel center. They're Austin's favorites. I'll wrap up some for you. It will only take a minute. Would you like a cup of coffee while you wait?"

"I'm fine. Thanks."

She disappeared through a doorway behind the counter and he walked closer to the display cabinet, wondering for a moment what it would be like to have someone care about his favorite preferences besides the people he paid to care.

The café tables near the front corner of the store were

filled with an older couple, a group of teenagers and two mothers with younger children. Sparkling holiday lights hung across the exposed brick on the far wall and snow-flakes dangled from the ceiling. Holiday music played softly in the background. A teenager came out from the back to help a customer who approached the counter. Liam moved out of the way, although he couldn't quite take his eyes off the pastries and treats that filled the display.

"Do you have a favorite?" Katie stood next to him, a brown bag tied with red ribbon in her arms.

"I'm not much for sweets," he answered automatically.

"He says to the bakery owner," Katie finished.

Liam gave a startled laugh, unused to good-natured teasing. "Lemon bars," he amended. "They're probably not popular this time of year, but I like lemon bars."

"I'll remember that." Katie slipped behind the counter.

"How long have you owned the bakery?"

"My grandmother left it to me when she passed a few years ago."

"I'm sorry for your loss."

She nodded. "I was lucky to have her in my life. Every kid needs someone to give them unconditional love. She was it for me."

"Ruth was my nanny, but she was the closest thing I had."

"Oh, she loves you all right. Have you seen her scrap-book?"

Liam's stomach dipped. "What scrapbook?"

"The one with every clipping and article she could find that mentioned your name. She used to have the local librarian save the old finance and business maga-zines for her. She was so proud of everything you did, used to brag about you like you were her own."

Liam felt his mouth drop open as a swarm of emotions went through him at the same time. Disbelief, gratitude and an overwhelming sense of loss. He'd kept his distance from Ruth for so long while she was collecting stories about him.

Katie's smile was infinitely gentle. "I'm going to put in one of my mini pecan tarts. You'll need a cold-weather favorite, and it's my personal mission to make everyone in town a fan of my bakery."

The bell rang and another group came into the store, pulling off scarves and hats as they did.

"I haven't talked to one person in town who doesn't love this place." He took the bag she set on the counter. "Besides I'm only here through the holidays, not regular customer material."

"I heard you may be moving your new company here."

All the emotion, the newfound affection for Crimson he'd been feeling dried up, like an errant drop of water in the desert. It didn't stand a chance against the harsh light of the truth. The only reason Katie Garrity was being nice to him, the only reason anyone in this town gave a damn, was because they saw dollar signs when he walked into the room.

He was used to it, so why did it rankle him so much? Maybe that's all he truly had to offer anyone. If that was the case, did it matter if he set up LifeMap in Crimson or some other town?

As if he'd summoned it, his past came walking into the bakery at that moment in the form of Logan Travers. He was bigger and broader than he'd been in high school, his long arm draped casually around the shoulders of the polished and surprisingly straitlaced-looking woman next to him.

Katie looked stricken for a second before pasting on another bright smile. She waved to Logan and the woman.

"Olivia, I don't think you've met Liam Donovan."

The woman's dark eyes remained focused on Liam, but she wrapped a hand around Logan's waist and squeezed, as if calming a wild animal.

"Welcome back," Olivia said. "I'm sure Ruth is very happy to see you again."

"She might be the only one," Liam said, keeping his gaze on Logan, who stared right back.

"How much do I owe you for the brownies?" Liam asked Katie.

"They're a gift to Ruth."

He glanced at her, brows raised. "I can pay."

She laughed, another surprise. "I'm well aware of that. From what I understand, you could pay for half the town without noticing a dent in your bank account."

"Katie," Olivia whispered. One side of Logan's mouth quirked.

Liam found himself returning the bakery owner's smile. "Then why comp me? Why not take advantage of my bank account while you have the chance?"

Katie shrugged. "Because some things are more important than money. The fact that you are here for Ruth this Christmas is one of them."

Olivia turned to Logan. "I'm going to talk with Katie about the order for the Winterfest reception. Would you get me a cup of tea?" She reached up to stroke his cheek and Liam noticed a diamond band on her left hand. Logan's wife. Not who he would have picked for the wild and reckless boy he'd known Logan to be.

"Earl Grey?" Logan asked, dropping a soft kiss on his wife's temple.

With a nod from Olivia, the two women walked away. "Could we talk outside for a minute?" Liam asked.

Logan's eyes widened a fraction, and then he gave a sharp nod and led Liam toward the door. If he was going to have this conversation, Liam figured it would be better to do it outside the bakery, with its cheery decor and warm atmosphere. What he had to say to Logan wasn't cheery or warm.

Tucking the bag under his arm, he welcomed the rush of cold air. The sidewalk was crowded with holiday shoppers, the buildings along the main street glowing in the pale afternoon light. This would be a good town for LifeMap, he thought, despite his complicated history here. Unfortunately, the conversation he was about to have would almost certainly blow that kernel of a plan to bits.

Logan walked several paces, out of sight from the bakery window, then turned. "Whatever it is you want to say to me—"

"I'm sorry," Liam interrupted.

Logan stilled for a moment, then tucked his hands into the pockets of his thick corduroy jacket. He didn't respond, or throw Liam into a wall, which was a pretty good sign as far as Liam was concerned.

"I should have said it ten years ago or at any point since then, but I'm telling you now. You lost your sister that night and I'm sorry I was there, that I had anything to do with her death." He drew in a breath, the cold air burning his lungs. "I'm sorry I didn't stop her from getting into that car."

Logan rocked back on his heels, glancing up at the gray sky for several long moments. A cloudy day in Colorado was a rare thing, even in the winter. Liam thought it fit the tenor of this conversation perfectly.

"I blamed a lot of people for the accident that killed

Beth," he said finally. "My parents, my brothers and myself most of all." His piercing blue eyes, as cloudy as the sky above, met Liam's. "For a while I blamed you, too. Plus the idiot who was driving."

"I shouldn't have let it happen. I'd been drinking—we'd all been drinking—but I wasn't so far gone that I didn't know better." He crossed and uncrossed his arms over his chest, pain from the memory of that night slicing through him. "I'd had a fight with my dad that day, and Natalie was busy with her grandma, who was really sick. I just wanted to forget everything, to obliterate it with alcohol."

"You and Beth had that in common," Logan said quietly.

"If I could change what happened, trade places—"

"No." Logan cut him off, shaking his head. "You were the only one to survive the accident. That's a lot of guilt to carry around for a decade. Things happened the way they did. No one can change the past. I wish it would have been different, but I'm done with blame and guilt. They were my relentless companions for a lot of years, but I've left them behind."

"I'm glad," Liam said honestly. "I'm guessing your wife has a lot to do with that."

"It took me a long time to believe I deserved to be happy, that I was more than what people around here thought of me."

"From what Jase has told me, you're now the go-to contractor for historic remodels in the area."

Logan shrugged his broad shoulders. "I do all right. Turns out I was a lot harder on myself than anyone else." One blond brow lifted. "Sound familiar?"

Liam barked out a laugh. "It's a bit of a different story with me. I was always an outsider in Crimson."

"Not to Ruth. Or Natalie." He held up a hand when Liam would have argued. "I don't particularly care whether you stay or go. Although I will say that Natalie has been a good friend to my wife, and I like my wife to be happy. But if you do decide to look seriously at Crimson, let me know if you need help with locations or buildings. I've got some contacts around the area."

"Thank you." The two words seemed inadequate, but they were all Liam could manage.

Logan nodded. "I'm going to bring Olivia that tea." He went to step around Liam, then paused. "A few of us are going out to my brother's ranch for dinner Wednesday night. They're having a pre-Winterfest party. If you're available, come by around six. Jase will be there, and Noah Crawford is coming up from Denver."

"I haven't seen Noah since high school," Liam answered. "We played football together for a year." He toed the sidewalk with one boot. "Is Natalie invited?"

"Always to the ranch, but she doesn't usually make it unless she's off work. That woman works more than anyone I've ever seen." He gave Liam the barest hint of a smile. "If you can convince her to take a break, everyone would love to see her."

"She isn't… I don't…" Liam stammered then stopped himself. "I'll try," he answered simply. Logan nodded and walked back to the bakery.

Liam took a deep breath, realizing a weight had been lifted from his shoulders. Maybe this town wasn't such a bad place for him after all.

Chapter Nine

"Mom, come down here." Austin's voice was pitched high with excitement. "You've got to see this."

Natalie took one last look in the mirror. She pulled her hair back, feeling a little stupid that she'd curled it. They were just putting up Christmas decorations, no reason to wear her hair in anything but her normal practical ponytail. But after straightening her cherry-red sweater, she flipped her hair over her shoulder. It was even stupider to waste a decent-hair day because of nerves.

She pinched her cheeks and turned for the stairs, glancing back at the mirror one more time. Her dark jeans were tucked into knee-high boots and she hoped she looked casual, not as if she'd gone to great lengths to get ready this evening. For most women, jeans and a sweater were probably daily attire, but she spent most days in scrubs or sweatpants, so it felt as though she was Cinderella getting ready for the ball.

"Mom!" The cry was louder this time, and Natalie ran down the steps and to the front door, then stopped short.

"What the…"

Two huge trucks were parked in the driveway and a team of six men unloaded boxes and cartons onto the front yard. Liam's black SUV pulled up behind them and he climbed out, a huge grin on his face as he met her gaze.

"What's all the commotion?" Ruth came to stand next to Natalie. Her eyes widened as three of the men pulled a wire snowman out of the truck that was well over six feet tall.

"Look at all this." Austin jumped up and down on the front porch. "It's our very own winter wonderland. There's more decorations here than at Winterfest."

Liam came to the edge of the porch. "I wanted to give you the biggest, brightest Christmas you've ever seen," he said to Ruth.

Austin looked back over his shoulder. "It's so awesome. Right, Ms. Ruth?"

Natalie saw the older woman look between Liam and Austin. "Are these my decorations?" Her voice was small and confused.

"Liam got them for you, Ruth." Natalie put her arm around the woman's bony shoulders. "It was a surprise."

"I have colored lights," Ruth said, pointing to the strands of soft white lights one of the workers had just plugged in near the side of the house. "Those aren't my lights."

Natalie glanced at Liam out of the corner of her eye and saw his smile drop. "We'll put colored lights on the tree," she said quickly. "Remember your tree with the snow on the tips? We're going to hang ornaments on that tonight."

"And colored lights?" Ruth asked, her brow knitted in concern.

"You bet."

Ruth nodded, her gaze taking in all the boxes as she rubbed her hands up and down her arms. "It's cold out here. I'm going to sit by the fire. *Wheel of Fortune* is on now."

"Austin, walk Ms. Ruth back to the family room."

Her son started to protest, then caught her eye. "Can I come back out when they've got it set up?"

"Yes, if you put on a coat and boots. Ruth is right. It's cold tonight."

The older woman started down the hall as Natalie motioned Austin to follow. "The decorations are cool, Liam," she said as he entered the house. "She's going to love them once they're put up."

"Should I have them take everything away?" Liam asked when they were alone. His mouth was a tight line, a muscle ticked in his jaw. "Did I mess this up, too?"

She could have told him "yes," accused him of trying to throw his money around to impress them all. That would have ended whatever was bubbling between them, cut the connection for good. It would be the easy thing to do, the way to protect her heart from being hurt again. To keep her life orderly and controlled, just the way she'd crafted it for so many years.

But she knew that wanting to show off wasn't what motivated this bit of extravagance. The light in his eyes when he got out of the car, the excitement that bounced off him was just like Austin's. He'd wanted to make his nanny happy, pure and simple. It was an unspoken fact that this might be the last Christmas Ruth would spend at her beloved farm, and Natalie knew Liam wanted to make sure it was one she wouldn't forget, no matter how age and illness eventually ravaged her mind and body.

The fact that it hadn't worked out the way he'd planned broke her heart for him. When she looked at him now she saw a little boy who wanted his parents' love and approval but never got it. Who'd been sent to a military academy and expensive boarding schools and finally to live with a woman who wasn't even a member of his own family so that his needs didn't interfere with the lives of the people who'd brought him into the world.

She took a step closer to him, lifted her hand to the back of his neck. The muscles corded there, rigid and inflexible and she began to massage them gently. "Let them put up the decorations, Liam. We'll do the inside of the house with the things she remembers."

"She doesn't want this," he snapped, the bitterness in his voice at odds with the way his body swayed closer to hers. He dropped his head to give her better access, making her smile a little. Liam was like a puppy, always wanting to be scratched and petted—at least once someone got beyond his defenses. A puppy hidden under a turtle's protective shell.

Natalie understood the instinct for self-protection, for not trusting anyone to have your best interests at heart. Ruth had been one of the few people Liam had let in and he was grasping for a way to make her happy.

"She wants you here," Natalie said. "She got out the scrapbook again this morning."

He jerked in response to her words. "Katie Garrity mentioned the scrapbook. Why haven't I heard about this before?"

"I thought you'd seen it."

He shook his head.

"Let me just say," she said with a harsh laugh, "that

Austin knows more about you than he does about his own father. Ruth whips that thing out every chance she gets."

He sighed, but his eyes softened. "She shouldn't do that."

"She loves you and she's proud of you."

"But she doesn't want my gaudy Christmas display?"

"We'll see what happens when these guys are done." She lowered her hand and wrapped it around his hard biceps, tipping her head to rest against his shoulder as they watched the men work in the fading light. "You can't make them stop now. Austin would be crushed."

"He's a really great kid, Nat. You've done an amazing job with him." He wrapped his arm around her waist, drawing her closer. "Your ex-husband is an idiot," he whispered against her hair.

"Preaching to the choir."

They stood there in comfortable silence for several minutes, until their breathing matched. She felt safe enveloped in the warmth of him. The heat of his body was like the perfect blanket warding off the frosty temperature. At least that's how it felt inside, as if she was lit from within thanks to her feelings for him.

The sound of tires on the gravel driveway broke the spell. A shiver passed through her and she tried to step away when Tanner parked and got out of his truck, two pizza boxes and a brown paper bag in his hands. But Liam didn't let her go.

"Hey, Tanner, would you grab the bag that's on the backseat of the SUV?"

"Sure thing, boss. Looks like the crew is going to turn this place into the North Pole in record time. Nice work."

"It makes me feel just like my father," Liam said, finally taking his arm away, moving to the edge of the porch. "Spending guilt money because I ignored her for so long. I always got the best birthday gifts. There were crazy, extravagant presents the years he and my mother forgot. The more belated my birthday celebration, the more over-the-top they went on things."

"That isn't what this is about."

Tanner bounded up the porch steps. "Do you want me to have them bring in the boxes for the inside?"

"No." Liam's fingers clenched around the porch rail.

Tanner glanced at Natalie. "We're going to use Ruth's decorations for the inside," she told him. "They're in the attic. I can get them down after we eat."

"Sounds good," he said, balancing all the food in one arm as he clapped a hand on Liam's shoulder. "This is going to be amazing out here."

Liam grunted in response. Tanner lifted his brows at Natalie, a question in his eyes. Certainly he was used to Liam's moods and gruffness. They should just go into the house and leave him to stew with his thoughts. But she couldn't desert him right now, watching a group of strangers lay elfin siege to the farmhouse out in the cold.

"Come on," she said softly. She placed her hand over his on the rail, loosening his fingers enough to lace hers with them. "Let's eat, then you can help me pull out her tree."

"The one with the fake snow sprayed on the branches?" He held her hand tightly as they turned for the house.

"I hope she has a singing Santa Claus," Tanner said, opening the door to lead them in.

"How did you know?" Natalie laughed, then gasped as Liam spun her around, pressing a quick, hard kiss to her mouth.

"Thank you for making this okay," he whispered.

And she realized it was. At this moment, everything in her life was okay, even holding hands with the man who once shattered her heart. Natalie didn't exactly believe in Christmas miracles, but even she had to admit the season suddenly seemed filled with a lot more magic.

"Do you think there's a show on cable dedicated to holiday hoarders?" Liam shoved another box toward the attic steps. The pile was huge.

Natalie pulled out an oversize plastic Santa from a far corner. "Some of this stuff creeps me out." She held the Santa in front of her, and Liam grimaced. Paint was chipped off the face, leaving the jolly old fellow looking like the victim of a flesh-eating virus.

"That can't come down," he said with a laugh. "Unless her theme is 'The Walking Dead Christmas,' Santa needs to stay hidden."

She giggled in response and shoved the figure behind a dresser. "I didn't realize her attic was so full."

"I definitely wouldn't have needed to bring in any extra decorations."

"In the end, she loved it."

That was true. By the time they'd finished the pizza and brownies, the guys he'd paid to decorate the outside of the house had finished. They'd waited until the sun had set completely, then bundled up and gone out to the front yard to view the display. Liam had felt like Clark Griswold, embarrassingly excited to flip the switch for the lights.

As worried as he'd been, it had turned out just how he wanted. White lights twinkled along the roofline and dangled like icicles over the eaves of the house, giving the whole place a festive glow. They'd set up two large inflatable displays, one of children building a snowman and the other of a family of penguins ice skating. It was a little hokey, but Ruth's eyes had lit up at the sight.

Once she'd been assured that all her beloved Christmas decorations were going to be used, Ruth had been happy, which was all Liam wanted in the first place. Tanner and Austin were downstairs in her family room now putting together the circa nineteen-seventy-something tree with the sprayed-on snow. Liam wasn't much for nostalgia. That would imply halcyon memories, which hadn't been a part of his youth. But the first glimpse of that tree had brought him back to the first Christmas he'd spent in Crimson during high school. Although there had been no extravagant gifts or globe-trotting trips, it had been one of his favorite holidays. He understood why Ruth's time-worn ornaments and decorations meant so much to her.

Lost in thought, he turned directly into Natalie with the box he held. She gave a muffled grunt as the sharp edge of the box's corner stabbed her in the stomach.

"Oh, Nat." He dropped the box behind him and put his hands on her arms. "Are you okay?"

"Fine," she said on a wheeze, still doubled over. "Just lost my breath for a second."

Glancing around, he moved her back a few steps to where an old love seat had been abandoned. Pulling off the sheet that covered it, he pushed her down as gently as he could.

"It's okay," she said again, leaning back against the faded cushions. Her fingers rubbed a spot on the center of her belly. "I should have been paying attention to where I was going. Or where you were going."

"My fault," he said, removing her hand and lifting the hem of her shirt.

"Liam." She swatted at him.

"Natalie." He covered her fingers with one hand and pushed her sweater up with the other. An angry red scratch marred the smooth skin of her stomach.

"This is not a big deal," she said, her voice sounding more breathless than it had a few minutes ago. He figured he might be to blame for that. Because suddenly the unheated attic was overly warm. "I was looking at your butt," she muttered, closing her eyes.

Liam tried to hide his grin. "Checking me out, huh?"

"Not the first or last time, I'm sure." She tugged at his fingers, but he didn't let go. Wondered why he'd ever let her go. "I got my karmic payback." She pulled her sweater down, but he kept his hand on her skin, unable to break the contact with her.

"You were the only one who ever mattered," he said softly, tracing circles on her stomach.

Her eyes fluttered open, and the heat in her gaze, the charge of electricity nearly melted him. Her lips parted, the pink tip of her tongue darting across their fullness.

He nearly groaned before lowering his head, using his tongue to lick the corner of her lips, then capturing her mouth with his. She was soft and tasted a little like brownies, sweet and rich. He let his fingers splay across her stomach as the kiss deepened, then moved them up to the curve of her breast.

Her answering moan made him crazy with need. She kissed him like her life depended on it, erasing every minute they'd been apart. His fingers found the peak of her nipple under the thin fabric of her bra, and she gasped when he squeezed the hard tip.

"Liam," she breathed against his mouth, arching into him. Any blood that was left in his head moved south. His desire for her so intense it almost drove him crazy. He needed some release, any release. Since he wasn't about to take her in the middle of a dusty attic, he decided that his best option would be to turn his attention fully to her. Natalie spent her life working and worrying. From what he could tell, she was wound so tight she might snap at any moment.

But not in this moment. Right now, she was loose and pliant in his arms, and he intended to take full advantage of it. As he kissed her, he let his hand drift lower, inside the band of her black yoga pants. She moved without realizing it, opening herself just enough for him to dip his fingers into her heat.

"Yes, there."

He smiled against her mouth, loving that she was bossy even in this instant.

Her hips bucked, her hands reaching up to thread through his hair. She made him wild with her need and he quickened his pace until her breath caught and he felt her body fall to pieces in his arms.

It made every moment of guilt he'd heaped upon himself in the past decade, every bitter thought, worth the pain. To bring her this pleasure made everything worth it. Why had he ever thought he was over her? Natalie would always be a part of him, no matter how things ended.

Chapter Ten

What the hell had she done? How had she let this happen?

As reality washed over her, cold and hard in its truth, Natalie tried to shift away from Liam, to distance herself from what they'd just shared, what he'd given her. Not that she didn't appreciate it. Life as a single mother with mountains of debt left no time for dating or romantic entanglements of any kind.

Plus, it was Liam. Who'd always known exactly how to hold her, touch her…and now…

Now she had to get away.

"Not so fast," he said, as if reading her mind. He draped his arm around her waist, pulling her closer up against the strong wall of his chest.

"We need to get back downstairs. What if someone comes looking? What if Austin—"

"One minute. One more minute isn't going to hurt."

She felt his heart beating, then noticed how hard he

still was…everywhere. "I'm sorry," she whispered automatically, turning to face him, moving her hand down the front of him. "Do you need me to—"

"No." He took her hand, lifted it, brushed his mouth across her knuckles. "I mean, yes, I'd love for you to touch me, Nat. Anytime. Anywhere. But that isn't what any of this was about."

She didn't want to look into his eyes, but couldn't help herself.

"This was about you," he said softly. "I want to take care of you."

She swallowed, feeling vulnerable, exposed and ripped wide apart by his words. It had been years since she'd trusted anyone to take care of her. And with good reason. Her life was a ticking time bomb, a cracked dam with her finger in the hole, trying to stop the impending flood from washing her away. She'd kept everyone in her life at arm's length as a matter of self-preservation. Her ex-husband's manipulation had isolated her, made her wary of letting anyone in. What if Brad tried to take advantage of someone she loved? Even though she'd denied it, there was still a possibility Ruth had some contact with him, and Liam…

Liam would be a prize mark for someone like Brad.

She couldn't run the risk of Liam finding out how much baggage she carted with her wherever she went. But she wanted to, with every part of her. She wanted to reveal her fears, her anger—to share the burden of her failed marriage so she didn't have to shoulder the regret alone. Despite all the years he'd been gone, Liam was the one person she wanted to tell.

She opened her mouth to say the words as he brushed his finger along her cheek, tracing the dark circle under her eye that lack of sleep had put there. A noise from the bottom of the stairs broke the spell between them.

"Mom, Ms. Ruth wants to know if you found the box with the angel for the tree?" Austin's innocent voice called up.

Natalie scrambled off the couch, whirling to where light glowed from the floor below. "We've got it all, buddy." She picked up one of the boxes. "On our way down."

"Natalie." Liam's tone held a note of frustration. "What we started here isn't finished."

She remembered that about him. Liam had never liked being denied, and Natalie was a master of denial.

"What have we started?" she asked, the words coming out on a harsh breath. "What do you really think is going on here?" She gripped the edge of the box so tight her fingers ached.

"You and I—"

"Were finished years ago," she interrupted. "When you walked away from Crimson and I stayed. My life is here, Liam. It's small and contained, and I like it that way. I've been taking care of my son and me for a long time. I don't need or want help." Her voice cracked on the lie, but she didn't stop. "You are fancy light displays and crews of workers. I'm a few boxes of old decorations stuffed up in the attic. Those two things don't mesh."

"I'm stuck out in the cold while you're inside where it counts?" He practically spat the words, twisting the meaning of what she'd said.

No, she wanted to yell. *You're inside me, all around me. You always have been.*

"Thank you for tonight," she whispered instead. "All of it. It means the world to Ruth."

"And you, Natalie?" he asked, relentless. No wonder

he'd been such a success in his life. His focus was un-wavering. "What does it mean to you?"

Everything.

"I've got to get back down there, Liam," she answered and turned away, trying to catch her breath as she stumbled down the attic steps.

"I've got a meeting scheduled with the development committee of Crimson's town council. Tomorrow at nine." It was Sunday morning, and Tanner pushed a box with the words "Life is Sweet" on the top toward Liam. "They've got a proposal ready for you, outlining the tax breaks and other incentives the town is willing to offer. I think at least one county commissioner will be there, too."

"Cancel it." Liam didn't look up from his email. "And no more pastries in the house. I don't want to see another pink box from that bakery as long as I live."

"Are you kidding?" Tanner picked up the bakery box, cradling it like a beloved child. "I'm thinking of staying on in town just so I don't have to leave these bear claws behind."

"Then you'll be here by yourself. I'm flying to Vermont after Christmas. That's where LifeMap headquarters is going."

Tanner shook his head. "Since when?"

"Since now."

"What happened between you and Natalie the other night?"

Liam snapped shut the laptop. "Nothing. This has nothing to do with Natalie."

"Bull—"

"Vermont is a better fit."

"Crimson is the perfect fit." Tanner pointed a finger at him. "And not just for LifeMap."

"Don't." Liam got up, stalked to the counter and poured a third cup of coffee. It was only nine in the morning, but he hadn't slept worth a damn the past few nights. Ever since Natalie had walked away from him. "Don't act like you have some great insight into me. This is business, plain and simple."

"Your father called."

Coffee sloshed over the rim of Liam's mug. "Why did he call you and not me?"

"Because I'm more likely to answer."

"Does he know I'm in Colorado?"

His assistant ignored the question, opening the Life is Sweet box and pulling out a pastry.

"Tanner."

"He knows. He said something about you not being able to cut the apron strings from your nanny."

"Jackass," Liam muttered, although his father's comment still stung.

"He also mentioned that he's coming to Aspen for Christmas."

"I thought wife number five didn't like cold weather since it means she has to cover up her assets?" With every marriage, his father picked women who were younger and more surgically enhanced. Liam was pretty sure his father's latest wife was barely in her twenties. "Shouldn't they be headed to Hawaii or the Bahamas?"

Tanner didn't answer, instead taking a big bite of bear claw.

"What's going on?"

"I think he wants to spend Christmas with you," he said when he'd finished chewing. He picked up a napkin and wiped it across his mouth, mumbling something else as he did.

Liam couldn't have heard him right. "Repeat that."

"Donovan Enterprises is interested in acquiring LifeMap."

The coffee he'd just swallowed turned to acid in Liam's stomach. "No. Way."

"I told him you'd say that." Tanner gave an almost apologetic shrug. "He wants to meet with you personally."

"The company is barely off the ground. The developer has a prototype, that's all. He can't be interested in the company. The whole mission is a stretch for Donovan Enterprises, not what they usually fund at all."

Tanner just looked at him.

"It's me," Liam said, not disguising the bitterness in his tone. "He can't stand to have me out on my own. He never believed I could be a success without his backing, so he wants to make sure I'm not."

"I don't think he liked the Jerry Maguire way you resigned."

"It wasn't a manifesto," Liam muttered.

"You wrote an open letter to the board detailing the ways Donovan Enterprises needed to improve its business dealings, everything you'd found lacking in the company. I believe 'morally corrupt' were the words you used to describe your father."

"That's kind if you knew the words I was thinking in my head right now." Liam gripped the edge of the counter, then turned. "It was the only way I could make a clean break. He would have never let me go if I hadn't made everyone on the board so angry." He scrubbed his hand over his face. "I worked hard for Donovan Enterprises, made every deal I touched there a success. It was time for me to try something different."

"Not arguing," Tanner said, holding up his hands. "I followed you, remember?"

"And it's been good, right?" Liam realized how much the answer mattered and rushed on, "The work, I mean.

Creating a company, a product from scratch. I know there aren't as many five-star lunches and courtside seats from investors. The perks of working for LifeMap are pretty much—"

"Wrapped up in a pink box?" Tanner lifted the lid, stepping forward to wave it under Liam's nose. "This is as good as it gets as far as I'm concerned. We've been a team out of the gate, man. LifeMap is going to blow things out of the water and I'm stoked to be a part of it. You need to work out your issues with your father. There's no doubt about that."

"He isn't—"

"And you need to work out whatever crap is going on with you and Natalie."

"She doesn't—"

"And your hang-ups about this town."

Liam narrowed his eyes and grabbed an apple turn-over out of the box. "When did you become so damn insightful?" He bit into the flaky crust of the pastry and for a moment forgot about all his problems in the bliss of that perfect bite. Katie Garrity was a master baker, he knew that for sure.

"I've always been insightful." Tanner opened a bottle of water. "That's why you pay me the big bucks."

"Stop talking now." Liam closed his eyes. "You're ruining my moment in sugar heaven."

"To think a few minutes ago you were ready to deny yourself that bliss. It makes me wonder..."

Liam opened one eye, squinting at his longtime friend. "Spit it out."

"It's like you are willing to write off Natalie and the whole town because things are a little more complicated than you'd expected."

"A little?" Liam asked, both eyes on Tanner now. "You know my history with her…with this town."

"I sure as hell hope you're a different person than you were ten years ago. But if you keep running off in different directions every time things get hard, then you're never going to move forward on the path you actually want to take."

"I'm not running." Liam tossed the uneaten half of turnover back into the box, his appetite spoiled by the unbidden truth. "You're forgetting that Crimson was the unwanted detour. I'm here because something is happening to the money I've put aside for Ruth. Something beyond her care, obviously, because other than the doctors, she still lives like it was twenty years ago." He pressed his palms to the counter, letting the cool of the granite seep into his skin. "Do we have any more information on that?"

"Unfortunately, no." Tanner shook his head. "The manager at the bank has her signature on the withdrawal slip, but you say she has no memory of taking out the money."

"Not that she'll tell me. But it's difficult to know what she actually remembers at this point. The money came out in chunks, so either she's got it hidden someplace or—"

"Someone is forging her signature?"

"It makes sense, but there aren't many people who have that kind of access to her."

"Natalie does," Tanner offered, almost reluctantly.

Liam took a last drink of coffee and put the mug in the sink. "She says she didn't take the money. But…" He paused, not wanting to say the thought out loud. "She's hiding something. There's more to the story than she's sharing. What about the other nurse?"

"Nothing suspicious there, but I'll keep looking. Have you found out anything more from Ruth?"

"I tried pushing her to give me better answers, just a bit, and she got very agitated." Liam paced to the edge of the kitchen. "She told me if I don't trust her with the money, to just take it back. Like that's the point."

"We'll figure it out. But don't give up on this town yet for LifeMap. At least meet with your friend Jase and the other town council members. Locals may be more willing to help out if you keep things friendly."

"The story of my life," Liam snapped. "People being nice because they want something from me."

"You're the one who wanted to come here, Liam."

"I know. I thought it would be easier." He held out a hand when Tanner's brows shot up. "Not one more word about me walking away when things get difficult. Or I'll fire you."

Tanner just laughed. "Good luck with that."

Liam grabbed the laptop off the counter and headed for the home's office. Sunlight streamed through the floor to ceiling windows, reflecting off the gilded mirror on the far wall. The furniture in the house was formal and pretentious. He hated it. He hated how it felt impersonal, valuable but lacking any sort of character or substance. A lot like his life.

He missed being at the farmhouse when he wasn't there, the cozy warmth of it. The smell of the fireplace, the White Shoulders perfume Ruth had been wearing since he was a kid, the sound of Austin's video games and Natalie humming as she went about her work. It felt like a home. Liam realized what he wanted more than anything was to experience that feeling of home while he was in Crimson.

He had an idea of how he could gain more access to Ruth, to take a closer look around and see if he could find the start of a paper trail that might lead him to answers about the money he'd given her. Natalie wouldn't like it, but he found that made the plan all the more appealing. He liked her off balance. Hell, he liked her any way he could get her. He was tired of fighting the connection between them, and it was past time she stopped fighting it, too.

Chapter Eleven

It was almost eleven when Natalie parked her car in
front of the farmhouse, cursing the butterflies that flit-
ted across her stomach at the sight of Liam's big SUV
in the driveway.

She'd been asked to take on an extra shift at the senior
center and had arranged for Olivia to stay with Austin
and Ruth. She hated asking friends for favors, but right
before Christmas she needed the money more than her
pride. According to Olivia, Logan had gone to Crested
Butte overnight, so she'd been happy to keep busy. But
now Olivia's car was gone, so she knew she'd be facing
Liam alone.

Natalie half expected him to lay into her for shirking
her responsibilities with his former nanny. She couldn't
blame him for not quite trusting her since she hadn't yet
explained her whole situation to him. Guilt ate away at
her even though she hadn't taken the money. Natalie had
tried to talk to Ruth about whether she'd paid off Brad.

But Ruth continued to act as though she had no memory of Natalie telling her anything about the debt. She wanted to believe Ruth, but, other than speaking to her mother, Brad had left her alone for nearly three months. That was a record and Natalie was almost able to sleep through the night without waking up in a cold sweat, worried about her ex-husband's next demands on her.

She glanced at the barn's workshop before walking toward the house. She had to finish up a few bracelets tonight, but first needed to check on Austin and Ruth and figure out why Liam was there instead of Olivia.

The house was quiet as she walked in, peaceful in its silence and shadows. Natalie took a breath and walked into the den, where she could see the light of the television glowing blue in the darkness.

She stopped short in the doorway at the sight of Liam stretched out on the couch, arms crossed over his chest, fast asleep. Her heart sped in rhythm as her body had its annoyingly familiar reaction to him. Stupid body with its heat and flush. She started to clear her throat then stopped, swept up in memories as she watched him.

Asleep and unaware of her presence, he looked softer, younger. More like the boy she'd fallen in love with so many years ago. A lock of dark hair fell over a forehead smooth without lines from worry or anger. Worry about Ruth and anger at Natalie. She deserved it, she knew, for her fear and cowardice. And so much more. But it didn't seem to matter now. Now that he wasn't looking at her with so many tangled emotions, she could let go of her own regrets for a moment and just relish being with him.

Because even asleep, Natalie could feel Liam's energy and the connection between them that didn't seem to break, no matter how she pushed and stretched it. She inched closer to the couch, glancing at the TV as she did.

One of the Marvel Comics movies played, making her smile. Liam always had a thing for superheroes.

Should she leave him there? Clearly he'd sent Olivia home and settled in to wait for her himself. Would Tanner worry if he didn't come back to the house or would the assistant assume he'd gone into town and found some young snow bunny willing to invite him to share her bed for the night? She wished she could be that woman, casual and willing, but Natalie had always felt older than she was.

Except when she'd been with Liam.

Unable to help herself, she reached out a finger to brush away the stray hair. In an instant a strong hand gripped her wrist, tugging her so that she fell with a grunt onto the back cushions of the couch.

"First you were checking out my butt in the attic. Then you're sneaking up on me while I sleep." His voice was rough, pitched low. It did wicked, hot things to her insides.

"I like you when you're asleep," she muttered, trying not to breathe in the scent of him. Trying to keep her bones from melting right into the sofa. "Sometimes more than when you're awake."

"Ahh, Natalie," he said on a soft laugh. "You never give an inch."

"I'm not the one with only a few inches to give." She shifted, letting her knee drive against him, wanting to make him as bothered as she felt in this moment.

He laughed again, turning so that she sank onto the cushions and they faced each other. "Don't make me prove you wrong," he whispered.

Her body burned at all the points it touched his. His face fell into shadows, but they were so close she could still see him clearly. He reached behind him toward the coffee table, and a moment later the television flicked off, leaving a thin strand of moonlight the only light in the room.

His finger traced her skin, starting at her forehead and working its way down the side of her face to her neck and throat, stopping at the collar of her scrub shirt.

"Working late," he murmured.

"The day isn't over yet," she answered, trying not to be carried away by his touch. "I have jewelry to finish tonight. Why are you here?"

"I came to see Ruth." A wisp of a smile played across his lips. "And you." His finger brushed the tender flesh of her earlobe. "I can't seem to stay away from you, Nat."

"You managed it for ten years."

"Do you think I ran away?" His voice was soft but there was steel in his tone.

"I think you left." Her voice sounded breathless to her own ears. It was hard to concentrate on anything with him so close, with his skin on hers. "Walking. Running. Does it really matter? The result was the same."

"After the accident that killed Beth, I didn't think—"

"Shh." She placed her fingertip on his mouth, silencing him. "We both think too much, Liam. I'm tired of thinking, my brain on overdrive all the time. I'm sick of guilt and blame and regret. I just want…"

"What?" He leaned closer, so close his breath feathered against her cheek. "What do you want, Natalie?"

Where to start with a list of what she wanted? How to even begin? She'd buried her wants and needs for so long, ignored them until she barely remembered that she'd ever had dreams for herself. "I want to feel something," she whispered, wiping her cheek on the sofa cushion to hide a stray tear that fell. "I want to feel again."

His gaze was at once tender and fierce, the dichotomy of Liam Donovan and what had always fascinated her. "I can help with that," he answered with total confidence and gently pressed his lips to hers.

She grasped at his shoulders and shifted closer. The kiss deepened, but not the pace. He sipped at her, nipped and licked, as if they had all the time in the world. As if he knew that her emotions in this moment were so brittle that she might break apart if he pushed her. Leisurely, his hands traveled down her body, pulling up the hem of her shirt so that he could touch her back.

Bit by bit, Natalie began to feel. She allowed herself to really enjoy what was happening, not the frenzied desire of when they were in the attic. She slipped into this passion as if it was a warm bath, enveloping her. It enveloped her tired muscles and weary bones, soothing her. This was true intimacy, the two of them without their defenses.

For a moment, panic flared and she placed her hand on his chest, ready to push him back before she gave away too much. Before she let him fill all the secret, lonely places she cradled deep inside. But she could feel his heartbeat pounding, although his motions remained gentle.

Another contrast and one that allowed her to believe she was safe, at least for the moment, in Liam's arms. She savored the feeling that awakened inside of her— a pinprick at first. Then it was as if the dam broke and everything she'd denied herself for so long flooded through her in waves.

She tugged at his long-sleeve Henley and he shrugged out of it before pulling her scrub top and the T-shirt she wore underneath it over her head. He lifted her, flipping onto his back and bringing her down against him, skin to skin. She'd forgotten the sensation of a man holding her, his hands roaming up her back and flicking open the clasp on her bra.

"Lift up," he whispered. "I want to see you, Nat."

She hesitated, again worried that the body she had now wouldn't match his memories of the girl he'd known.

"Who you are now?" he said, as if reading her mind. "Let me see you."

Because it was mostly dark in the room and his voice held such a note of reverence, she sat up. The bra straps slipped off her arms and he curled one finger under the lace edge and tossed it aside. His hands cupped the weight of her breasts and he lifted his head at the same time she bent forward, taking the hard tip of one in his mouth.

Natalie groaned with pleasure, which turned into a self-conscious laugh as Liam whispered, "You are so beautiful," against her skin.

He leaned back to look into her eyes. "I say you're beautiful and you laugh?"

His gaze searched hers.

"You don't have to whisper sweet nothings to me. This is enough." She awkwardly gestured to the muscles rippling across his skin. "More than enough."

"It's not nothing." He sat up, shifting so she was next to him on the couch. "You. Are. Beautiful."

She placed her hand over her chest, not to hide from him, but because her heart suddenly felt as if it might float away. It was light and sweet, like carnival-spun cotton candy. She felt as though she shed a hundred pounds and years of worry in that moment. "I want you, Liam," was all she could think of to say. She lifted his hand, pressing it against her skin along with her own. "I want this now."

His eyes tracked to the door leading to the hallway.

"Austin and Ruth sleep like the dead," she quietly assured him.

"Thank God," he said on a choked laugh. He leaned

forward and kissed her again, pushing her back along the couch. His fingers went to the waistband of her scrub pants. He pulled them, along with her underpants, down over her legs. Cool air brushed her sensitized skin and she drew in a shuddered breath, too on edge, too ready to even be self-conscious. Then he stood and unbuttoned his jeans, pulling a condom out of the wallet in his back pocket before shoving them off. He was perfect from head to toe, a sculpted chest and lean hips. Her head buzzed with wanting.

A moment later he was over her, his kiss more intense, full of the same need Natalie felt to her core. His hand reached between them, finding her center, as he caught her gasp with his mouth. Instinctively, she parted to give him better access. But as the pressure built, she realized she didn't want this to happen without him. After so many years of denying herself pleasure, of focusing on making it through each day, this act of abandon felt wild and indulgent, much like her feelings for Liam had always been.

She reached for his hand, pulling it away. "Together, Liam. Now."

He shifted again, fit himself to her, and then they were joined. All the sensations she'd held back crashed together at once, a mix of light and sound in her head, almost overwhelming in its intensity. So she held on to Liam, locked her gaze on his. The emotion in his gray eyes grounded her, allowed her to feel without being afraid of losing herself. For someone who spent most of her life being afraid of something, it was a revelation for Natalie. Letting go of her fear was the best medicine she could imagine.

I love you.

The words were on the tip of her tongue, but she didn't

say them. She might be having a moment, but that didn't mean she was going to admit it to Liam. He held her as they moved together, as if she were precious, as if she would always be safe inside the warmth of his embrace. The pressure built, each thrust exquisite torture for her. She hitched in a breath, then whispered his name as she broke apart. A moment later she felt him shudder, and he buried his head in the crook of her neck.

I love you.

Liam bit down on his tongue, hard, to keep from saying the words out loud. Maybe he'd never stopped loving her. Their time together had been short and they'd been so young. When he left Crimson, he'd blamed his heartache on the guilt over the accident, not the pain of being rejected by one more person he loved. That had been too much to process, so he'd shoved it aside, convinced himself that all they'd had together was a teenage fling.

He couldn't ignore the truth any longer. Being with Natalie in this moment was the first time since he'd left Crimson he'd been truly content. He held on to her until his breathing slowed and he could regain control of the storm inside. He'd put himself on the line for her once and couldn't stand the thought that she might hurt him again. Would not risk that, especially when he still believed there were secrets between them.

As soon as the thought appeared in his mind, he felt her pulling away. Not physically; she continued to stroke her delicate fingers down his back. But he could almost see her rebuilding her walls as they lay there. Maybe that was better. It would make it less complicated when he left, at least that's what he told himself. The splitting pain in his chest told a different story.

"So that was a nice way to wake up from a nap," he said softly, dropping a kiss at the hollow of her throat.

It was better for both of them to keep this moment light. Easier than the alternative. He didn't want to fight with her tonight, wouldn't risk tainting what had just happened between them.

He felt her jerk a little in surprise, wondered what she'd expected from him. Thought of all the reasons he'd given her to not trust him.

She moved slowly, shifting off him. "Hopefully it will give me some energy for another late night."

He moved his legs to give her room on the sofa. She bent forward and tossed his shirt and jeans to him. "Don't look at my butt."

"You started it."

She smiled, just a little, but that was enough for him. If she was freaked out by what had happened, she was handling it well.

Getting dressed, he watched as she grabbed her things and moved to the far side of the room behind the couch.

"What are you doing?"

"There's more privacy over here," she said, her voice muffled by the shirt she pulled over her head.

"Privacy?" He chuckled. One minute she was wrapped around him like a pretzel and the next she needed privacy to put on her clothes. Her contradictions never ceased to fascinate him.

"You never answered my question. What are you doing here so late? Olivia would have stayed."

"I'm staying," he answered. "Here, I mean. At the farmhouse for a few days. Until Christmas probably." He pulled his shirt over his head, not exactly surprised that she was standing in front of him when he finished.

"You absolutely aren't staying here." She pointed one finger at him, waving it back and forth.

"In the old office above the barn, actually," he clarified. "I had a bed moved in tonight along with my things."

"What about your house in town?"

"Tanner will stay at the rental."

"Why would you want to give up that place and come here?"

He wiggled his eyebrows at her, patting the couch as he did. "I can think of at least one benefit."

Without hesitation, she kicked him in the shin. Hard.

"Oww. What the hell, Natalie?" He jumped up from the couch and hobbled to the end of the room as he sucked in deep breaths. She'd put back on her work clogs, so that kick meant business.

"What the hell, Liam?" she mimicked. "You could have mentioned that tidbit of information before. I'm not your friend with benefits, you know."

"I know." He held out his hands, palms up. "I was joking."

"Not funny. You can't stay here."

"I can and I'm going to." He lifted his leg, rubbing his shin with his palm. "This isn't about you."

She crossed her arms over her chest and grunted.

He had it bad when she made a grunt sound sexy.

"It's not entirely about you. I need to figure out what happened to Ruth's money."

"So you're here to watch me?" She threw her hands into the air. "I can't believe I just got naked with you."

"No way." He dropped his leg and stalked toward her. "Don't bring that into this. I'm not here to watch you." He paused then added, "Exactly."

He was pretty sure her head was about to start spinning. "Exactly?"

"I'm here to watch Ruth. To watch out for her. You knew that from the start."

"I told you I didn't steal the money."

"I believe you."

"If you only…" She stopped, tilted her head. "Did you say you believe me?"

"I'm not the enemy, Natalie." He was close enough now to reach out and trace his finger along the beard burn on the side of her neck. He'd put that there, marked her. It gave him a burst of primal satisfaction. "If you tell me what's going on—"

"You said you believed—"

"I also think there's more to the story than you're sharing."

She glanced at the doorway leading to the hall as if she might make a run for it. "I need to work on the jewelry or I'll never get to sleep tonight."

He waited for her to say more, but she grabbed her coat off a chair and turned.

"I'll walk you over there." He shoved his feet into a pair of gym shoes and followed her.

"No need." She threw the words over her shoulder, not slowing her pace.

"I'm heading to the barn anyway." He took his jacket from the row of hooks near the front door and followed her out into the night. The air was so crisp and cold it almost took his breath away. A thousand stars twinkled in the clear sky above them, the only sound the crunch of snow under their feet. He didn't want this rigid distance between them. He wanted to pull her into his arms and kiss her until she was pliant again.

"How's the search for a new headquarters?" she asked suddenly, glancing at him from beneath her lashes.

"Fine…good," he stammered.

"Are you bringing the company to Crimson?" She took a set of keys out of her pocket as they got nearer to the barn.

The question stunned him, especially after the comment he'd made to Tanner about Vermont. "I'm meeting with some people from town council and the county tomorrow," he offered, hedging on a direct answer.

"I'm not the only one holding back." The smile she gave him was sad.

It amazed him that she could read his intentions so easily. He wouldn't have gotten nearly as far in business if everyone was as perceptive as Natalie.

She turned the key in the lock, opened the side door of the barn and flipped on a switch to bathe the mudroom in fluorescent light. He squinted against the abrupt change. "Is this how it's always going to be for us?" he asked quietly. "Neither of us willing to budge once we draw a line in the sand?"

"I don't know, Liam. I want…"

He held his breath, wondering if this was the moment that would change what was between them.

She shook her head, as if whatever she had to tell him was too raw. "Everything I want now is for Austin. He's my priority."

"He's lucky to have you." He gestured to the workshop behind her. "Do you want some company while you work?"

She rose up on tiptoes and kissed the edge of his mouth, drawing away before the kiss could take off into something more for either of them. "Thank you, but I get pretty involved in the jewelry when I'm making it. Go to bed, Liam. I'm sorry I reacted the way I did about you staying here. You have every right to be near Ruth. Having you around has made her so happy."

"She deserves as much happiness as I can provide. Good night, Nat." He walked up the steps to his makeshift bedroom, but it was hours before he finally fell asleep.

Chapter Twelve

Running in five different directions while juggling a half dozen balls in the air seemed to be the story of Natalie's life. She'd taken off early from her shift at the senior center the next day to drive to Aspen to pick up a skateboard she'd specially ordered for Austin for Christmas. A wreck on the two-lane highway that ran between the two towns delayed her return. She'd been about to call one of her friends when her cell rang. It had been Liam, who had immediately sensed something was wrong and offered to pick up Austin from school.

It was difficult enough for Natalie to rely on her friends so she'd said no. He'd insisted. Now, an hour after Austin's school let out, she found a parking spot on Crimson's crowded main street and dashed toward the Life is Sweet bakery, where Liam had texted her from a few minutes ago.

She breathed a sigh of relief when she saw her son's dark head at a table near the window. Her feet stopped moving for a moment as she watched Liam and Austin together. Austin's wide smile was contagious, and Liam laughed at something he said then ruffled his hair, the same way she'd done so many times. Shoppers and tourists jostled her as they walked past. The middle of the sidewalk was no place to stand still the week before Christmas.

Stepping into the bakery, some of the tension in her back and shoulders eased. The deliciously sweet scents and warmth of Katie's shop were hard to resist.

"Hey, guys." She bent to kiss Austin's cheek, then smiled as Liam tilted his face toward her like a dare. Instead, she awkwardly patted his arm. "Sorry I'm late today, buddy." Her gaze met Liam's. "Thanks for getting him."

"My pleasure." He glanced behind her. "You should know—"

"Grandma's here, too," Austin announced, spooning up a bit of pecan pie. "Mom, you've got to try this."

He held it up for her, but Natalie's mouth had gone dry. "You eat it, hon," she managed.

"Sorry," Liam whispered, cringing a little. Trudy had that effect on people. "She saw us in the window."

"And what a cozy scene it was." Natalie turned as her mother sauntered up to the table, her penciled-in eyebrows almost hitting her hairline as she gave Natalie one of her patented death stares. "I haven't been in here since Katie's grandma owned the place. Prices have gone up. Two bucks for a cup of coffee? What a rip-off. But the food looks good."

"It's the best," Austin confirmed as Natalie worked to swallow the bile that rose in her throat. "I can't believe you haven't been here, Grandma. You work right around the corner. Mom and I come in for a snack every chance we get."

"Is that so?" Trudy pushed in next to Natalie, crowding her, making her head spin with the smell of old perfume and cigarettes. "Next time have her bring you by to visit me."

"I take him to the bar enough, Mom," Natalie said through clenched teeth. "If you want to see him more, we can make other plans."

"Plans that involve his father, I hope," Trudy muttered. "Not some virtual stranger." She threw a pointed look at Liam, who helped himself to a bite of Austin's pie.

"These might beat out Katie's brownies as your favorite, huh?" he asked, clearly implying knowledge of Austin's preferences in front of Trudy.

Natalie bit back a strangled laugh. Too bad the bakery didn't serve liquor. She could use some liquid fortification right about now.

"Liam's not a stranger, Grandma." Austin picked up a corner of crust as he spoke. "He and Mom are old friends. He invited me to the island where he has a house. It would be cool to go to the beach this summer. He even has a plane that would pick me up."

Natalie heard her mother's gasp. "Do you know how many private jets crash each year, Austin? And what happens when they go down?"

Austin shook his head, the chunk of crust suspended in the air.

"People die."

For a moment Natalie was as riveted as her son, compelled by the fervency of her mother's tone. She'd listened to Trudy's rants for as long as she could remember. She thought she'd outgrown her mother's ardent fears, but she felt her stomach churning at the thought of taking Austin on a trip anywhere. Which was how she'd ended up tied to Crimson her whole life.

"Fiery, painful deaths. You can hear their screams as the skin melts—"

"Mom!" Natalie grabbed Trudy's arm, yanking her hard. "That's enough."

"You can't let him go." Trudy grabbed her right back, her fingers twisting Natalie's arm under the fabric of her parka and thick sweater.

"We haven't made any plans." Natalie flinched against her mother's viselike hold.

"Mrs. Holt, this is my fault." Liam shifted in his chair as both Natalie and her mother turned to face him. "I talked to Austin about the beach. It seemed like a good way to forget about the cold temperatures as we walked downtown. But I would never put him in any danger. Austin or Natalie. I promise you."

Her heart gave an uneven beat as she watched the sincerity in his gaze. It took a special man to face her mother's brand of crazy and take responsibility for it. She wanted to reach out and touch him, to once again ground herself in his rationality.

Her mother leaned forward instead. "I know your type, Liam Donovan. You think you're so important. You come in here and make promises you won't keep, make my daughter believe she's better than she is. I know different, and so does my Natalie. I want no part of what you're selling."

Liam lifted his hands. "I'm not—"

"Austin, your father wants to see you for Christmas. He misses you very much and has lots of plans for the two of you. He's going to see your mother, too. They might—"

"Mom, stop!"

Trudy blinked several times, as if coming back to

herself. It was like her mother had gone to her own personal revival and been filled with a spirit, a mean and bitter spirit intent on battering down the foundation of Natalie's life. "I've got to get to work," her mother said. Without another word to any of them, she turned and walked away, the bells from above the door chiming merrily as she left.

Natalie wanted to run, too, but she sank down into the chair between Liam and Austin, her knees like jelly in the wake of her mother's outburst.

"Is Dad really coming to Crimson for Christmas?" Austin asked, his eyes wide. She couldn't tell if it was anticipation or apprehension in his eyes.

"I don't know, buddy," she answered honestly. "He hasn't contacted me, and I don't have any plans to see him. If he's talked to Grandma—"

"You need a piece of cake. Right this very minute." Natalie felt a hand envelope her shoulders. Katie stood next to her, sliding a small plate in front of her. "You okay?" her friend asked.

Glancing at Austin, Natalie forced herself to nod. "Thank you."

"I wish I could stay with you." Katie glanced over her shoulder. "But one of the girls called in sick and we've been busy all day. I can barely keep up." She turned to Austin. "How are you at boxing up cookies?"

He straightened. "I've never tried, but I bet I could be good."

"I bet you could, too," Katie agreed. "Can I borrow your son for about twenty minutes, Nat? I've got a couple of last-minute orders going out tonight."

"Sure." Natalie picked up a fork. "I'll be here with my cake."

Austin stood to go with Katie and placed his backpack on the empty seat. Natalie couldn't help but reach out and give him a quick hug as he left.

"It's okay, Mom. Grandma just gets excited sometimes."

His show of understanding made her insides ache. "You're the best, bud," she managed and watched him follow Katie into the back of the shop.

She let her chin fall to her chest, closed her eyes and concentrated on regulating her breathing. It was the same way she'd recentered herself from the time she was little and her mom would scream and yell about the horrors of the world outside Crimson. It had been a long time since she'd been on the receiving end of that toxic energy and it drained her.

At some point, she felt Liam take her hand in his. The pad of his thumb circled the sensitive skin on the inside of her palm. She almost pulled away, used to being alone in the aftermath of one of her mother's rants.

"So that just happened," she said quietly.

"I didn't realize it was so bad with her," he answered.

She glanced up, wiping away the tears she could feel clinging to her lashes with the sleeve of her coat. She would not cry, especially in front of him. "She's actually better than she used to be." She drew her hand away from his, not sure if she'd be able to get through this conversation while he was touching her. "She's had anxiety since I can remember, but it hit a high point in high school. She had about six months of full-blown agoraphobia when she wasn't able to leave the condo, even to get the mail or go to the grocery. I tried to convince her to see a therapist, but she didn't want anyone to know. Lou Bristol, who owns The Tavern, was nice enough to hold her job for her and eventually—when the money ran out—she got okay enough to go back to work."

"And you were taking care of her?"

"It was no accident I never invited friends over to my house," she said, trying to make a joke.

Liam didn't smile. "She fed you that garbage about the dangers of the big, bad world the whole time you were growing up?"

"I'm just glad the internet wasn't popular back then. Her ability to find photos of horrific plane crashes and images from natural disasters is kind of freaky."

"I'm not judging you for her behavior, but it had to be a burden."

"Most people don't know. She hides it behind her crusty attitude toward outsiders. I hide it with...everything I am." She clapped a hand over her mouth, aware of the vulnerability that statement revealed.

Liam only nodded. "I get that, too. Most people think my parents sent me to boarding school because that's where the offspring of families with wealth and privilege went. No one understands it was because my mother and father couldn't stand to have me around."

"That couldn't be the—"

"It's the truth," he interrupted. "Only Ruth knows, and now you."

His gaze locked on hers, wary and waiting. All she said was, "You didn't deserve that."

"It's part of why I never came to see Ruth after college. I felt like such a sellout, going to work for my dad after the way he'd treated me. I was embarrassed that I still wanted his approval and couldn't stand the thought that Ruth might call me out on my cowardice."

"She loves you, Liam. All she ever wanted was your happiness."

His chin hitched, acknowledging the words but putting an effective end to his sharing. She understood the need to reveal himself in bite-size pieces. It made the hurt more palatable. "What about your mom and Austin?" he asked.

"He's never alone with her." Natalie took a bite of cake, lifted it halfway to her mouth then set down the fork again. "She actually manages quite well these days. She has a route she takes between the condo, the grocery and the bar. It's like Crimson is her own mental biosphere. She feels safe as long as she sticks to the routine." She sighed. "Entering the bakery probably threw her off, then when Austin mentioned traveling…well, she's never had a meltdown like that in front of him."

"Are you making excuses for her?" Liam's voice was disbelieving. "She's got real problems, Nat."

"She's my mother, Liam. You think I don't know her issues?"

"Which explains a lot about your issues."

She bristled, hating to be called out on something she couldn't seem to change. "So I stay in one place. Are roots that are too deep better than no roots at all? We may have different ways of insulating ourselves from pain, Liam, but the result is the same." She sucked in a breath, forced herself to look him in the eye. "We remain alone."

He gave a hard shake of his head. "I don't want that anymore. I want to let people in. I want to let you in, Natalie."

"I'm not sure I can do that," she whispered. "I don't think I know how."

"One step," he told her, taking her hand again and brushing his mouth across her knuckles. "One step at a time. At least tell me you'll try while I'm here."

Could she do it? Could she make herself vulnerable to this man again? Risk being hurt? She knew it would take total honesty, revealing everything to him. They couldn't move forward without that. But right now she just wanted to enjoy the moment, the bright warmth of possibility rising up inside her. "Maybe it's time for a Christmas miracle."

She cupped his face in her hands and leaned forward, pressing her lips to his and refusing to care who might see her.

"That's a hell of a start," he said when she sat back.

She winked at him, feeling flirty and light for the first time in years. "We've got to start someplace."

"This was a mistake," Liam mumbled as he parked in front of the main house at Crimson Ranch.

Austin jumped out of the backseat, slammed the door behind him and ran up the steps to the big ranch house.

"What's wrong?" Natalie asked, placing her hand over his on the console. "Logan invited you himself."

"Dealing with one brother, even the biggest one, is different than having to face them all at the same time. Hey, guys," he said in a singsong voice, "sorry about your sister dying in my arms."

"Liam," she whispered, shifting to take his face between her hands. "Beth's death was an accident. Not your fault. No one's fault."

"I held that girl as she died, Nat."

"I can't imagine how awful that was. None of us can. I also can't imagine how Josh, Jake and Logan dealt with losing their sister." Her cool fingers felt like heaven on his overheated skin. "But they did. One day at a time. With baby steps."

He drew in a breath, letting the scent of her in the closed space of the truck's cab wash over him, cleanse the dark places inside him. "This feels like a long jump versus a baby step."

"I'll be with you the whole way." She leaned in even more and kissed him.

Too soon she drew back and opened her car door. "You ready?"

Ready to wrap his arms around her? Hell, yes. But he nodded and climbed out of the SUV.

The house was alight, warm and cheery with boughs of holly and ropes of pine garland strung throughout. *This is Christmas*, he thought, as Natalie led him to where voices could be heard in the back half of the house. They walked into an open family room and kitchen, a huge tree situated in front of the picture window. Stockings were hung off the mantel by the fireplace and the words from the popular holiday song popped into his head. There was no doubt those stockings had been hung with care. The big ranch house was literally bursting with love and cheer, so much so it made his teeth hurt.

One day at a time. The Travers brothers had rebuilt their lives one day at a time. It seemed almost impossible that he could ever get to this point. He knew he didn't belong here, in the midst of so much happiness. But true to her word, Natalie stayed by his side. She laced her fingers with his as the couples sitting around the tree turned.

"Natalie," a tall blonde squealed, walking from the kitchen to where they stood. "It's so good to see you."

Liam recognized her as Sara Wellens, the movie actress who'd just recently made a comeback in Hollywood. She also happened to be married to Josh, the middle Travers brother, and helped him run this guest ranch when she wasn't on a movie set. Her steps faltered for a moment as she noticed Natalie's hand in Liam's. Then her smile widened. She wrapped Natalie in a tight hug while Liam watched.

"I've been gone a couple of weeks filming," she said,

looking at Liam over Natalie's shoulders. "I miss my girlfriends when I'm gone."

"But not as much as she misses her husband," Josh called as he stood from the couch.

"You must be Liam," Sara said, holding out her hand. "I've heard all about you."

His stomach plummeted to the floor. "I shouldn't—"

"From what I understand your company is going to put Crimson on the map. Everyone in town is really excited to have you here."

"You might be giving Sara a run for her money as the local celebrity," Josh said as he joined their group. He held out a hand and Liam shook it, dumbfounded. He'd been so sure he was going to receive the cold shoulder from the other Travers brothers, at least until he apologized for what had happened to their sister.

"I'm happy to transfer the limelight to Liam," Sara said. "You be the star, Mr. Donovan."

"You'll always be my star, darlin'," Josh said, drawing his arm around Sara's shoulders.

"Join the party, you two." Sara motioned to the group in front of the fireplace.

"What can I get you to drink?" Josh asked.

"A beer," Liam answered. His throat felt as dry as sandpaper.

"Can you whip up one of those holiday cocktails for Natalie?" Sara asked, expertly batting her eyelashes at her husband.

"Of course."

"I'm okay with water," Natalie answered.

"One cocktail. It's frozen and strawberry." Sara wiggled her hips. "Guaranteed to put you in the holiday spirit."

Liam squeezed Natalie's fingers.

"One cocktail," she said after a moment.

Sara clapped her hands and pushed Josh toward the kitchen.

Natalie led Liam forward, introducing him to Olivia's half sister Millie, who was married to the oldest Travers brother, Jake. Jake had been in college when the accident occurred so Liam had never met him. He was the tallest of the three brothers, blond and lean. He also seemed the most serious. Liam knew he was a doctor and had moved back to Crimson last year.

Just as they shook hands a little girl ran up to Jake, pulling on his navy sweater. "Daddy, Daddy, I found a pair of reindeer ears under the tree." She held out a head-band with two felt ears sticking up from it. "Now we can both have antlers." The girl patted her own head that had similar ears sprouting out of it.

"This is my daughter, Brooke," Jake told Liam, straightening the girl's ears.

"Brooke, say hello to Mr. Donovan. He's a friend of Miss Natalie's."

"Hello, Mr. Donovan," she said in a soft, sweet voice. "I can try to find you some reindeer ears, too."

Liam almost laughed. "I don't think—"

He stopped when Jake cleared his throat. He looked over and was surprised to see the man sporting the reindeer antlers. Jake arched a brow, as if daring him to comment. Liam looked back at Brooke. "Sure. I'll take a pair of reindeer ears."

The girl gave him a bright smile. "Be right back," she said and disappeared again.

"Nice antlers," Josh said, joining them and handing Liam a beer.

He took a long pull on it.

"Be careful," Jake said quietly, "I've got a big red nose

hidden in my pocket. One more crack about my ears and you'll be playing Rudolph tonight."

Liam choked out a laugh, trying hard not to spit out his beer as he did. When Josh leveled a look at him, Liam held up one hand. "I'm just waiting for my ears."

"Smart man," Jake confirmed, and Liam relaxed a little. Somehow being game for his daughter's whims had smoothed the way with Jake Travers. Liam would wear the ears and nose if that's what it took.

"Is there anything you won't force the rest of us to endure to make Brooke happy?" Josh asked.

Jake pretended to think about it for a moment, then a grin split his face. "Nope."

"Are you close with your dad?" Josh turned to Liam, suddenly serious.

Normally Liam would give someone an ambiguous answer to that question. Maybe it was the beer or the general atmosphere at Crimson Ranch, but he found himself telling the truth instead. "We haven't spoken since I walked away from Donovan Enterprises. He's tried to reach out recently, but only because he wants to acquire LifeMap before the software launches. He's never had much use for me. That's how I ended up with Ruth in high school." He clamped his mouth shut, having given these two almost strangers more insight into his relationship with his father than he had to anyone in a long time.

Neither looked shocked. "Just remember to learn from that dysfunction when it comes time for you to be a father yourself," Josh told him.

Jake smiled. "What he's saying is don't be the same sort of jerk your father is. Do better. It's a big lesson."

Liam's gaze tracked to Natalie, standing near the dining room table with Sara and Olivia, before he forced it back to Josh. "I'm not—"

"Right," Jake said with a laugh, clapping a hand on Liam's shoulder. "We've all made that denial."

"Good luck," Josh added.

Liam shook his head. "Is this the part where you warn me that if I hurt her I'll have to answer to you?"

Josh tipped back his head and laughed. "We don't have to. If Natalie gets hurt, there won't be anything left for us once the women are done with you."

"Don't worry," Jake said. "If Josh, Logan and I can figure it out, you should have no problem."

Liam didn't know how to answer. He'd expected judgment and blame, but each of the brothers was welcoming in their own way.

A gust of cool air blew into the room as Logan opened the French doors that led to the patio. "The fire pit is ready," he announced, rubbing together his gloved hands.

"S'mores!" Austin yelled, jumping up from where he sat next to a teenage girl on the couch.

Jake's daughter ran in from the kitchen, her arms full of supplies. "I've got the marsh-smellows and chocolate," she cried.

"Slow down, Brookie-cookie," Jake said, catching her in his arms as she went past. "No running near the fire."

"You better come supra-vise me, Daddy."

"Only if you give me first dibs on the marshmallows," Jake said, carrying her toward the patio.

"No way," she said with a laugh.

Liam watched as everyone drifted out the back door.

Natalie held out her hand to him. "You can't say no to s'mores," she told him, crooking a finger in his direction.

The way he felt now, he couldn't say no to anything that involved her. Her eyes danced as he walked toward her, her cheeks alight with color. Maybe it was from the drink she'd had, but he liked to believe it had more to do with him—with them together.

She'd come to him late last night, after she'd finished work on her jewelry. He'd stayed awake as long as he could, debating whether to go down to her workshop when he'd heard her enter after putting Austin to bed. In the end, he'd decided against it. He knew the scene with her mother at the bakery had been difficult, and he didn't want to push her for more than she was able to give. He'd done that ten years ago and ended up losing her. *Patience*, he'd told himself. *Baby steps.* So he'd taken a cold shower and finally drifted off to sleep.

Only to wake up to Natalie's warm body sliding under the covers next to him, kissing him awake. The whole thing had been like a dream, the feel of her skin against his body, the scent of her shampoo and lotion surrounding him. He hadn't spoken, too afraid of breaking the spell. It had been enough to slip his hands under her sweater, to peel off her clothes and his own boxers before grabbing a condom from the nightstand and moving inside her.

"You're prepared," she'd whispered on a soft moan.

"Hopeful," he corrected, and she'd laughed into the base of his throat.

It was so easy, the two of them together in the intimacy of that moment. Moving with her, desire building as he touched her, made him forget everything else. The walls they both still hid behind, the things he wasn't willing to say to her, didn't want to ask her in return. All that fell away as he held her.

He had to choose whether to stay in Crimson and make it not only his home but headquarters for his company. Put the past behind him and go forward into a future he hadn't imagined.

"It's not that big of a decision."

Natalie's voice broke through his thoughts. She watched him from the doorway to the patio, an unsure smile on her face. She was talking about s'mores, unaware of the sliding slope his doubts created in his own mind. One step at a time, he reminded himself, and headed toward her.

Chapter Thirteen

The wind whipped up the snow, making it swirl around Natalie's head as she stood on the tiny front porch of her mother's apartment at the edge of town. She rang the doorbell, wondering for a moment how it had gotten to this point, where she felt like a stranger walking into the place where she'd been raised.

As she waited, her fingers straightened the old wreath on her mother's door. The berries were chipped, the fake pine bough a little smushed, as if it had been sitting up against something hard in her mom's small storage unit near the carport. She tried to reshape it into a perfect circle, as if accomplishing that might turn her life right again.

Trudy opened the door while Natalie was pulling on the edge of the wreath and the whole thing flipped off the nail that held it and crashed to the ground.

She bent to pick it up. "Sorry, the pine branches were crooked, so I was trying to make it round again."

"It's fine how it is," Trudy snapped, ripping the wreath from her hands and carefully rehanging it on the door. "Everything around here is great the way it is."

"Point taken," she said, following her mother into the house. The slightly burned smell of microwave popcorn filled the air. Her mother lived on popcorn and frozen dinners, had for as long as Natalie could remember.

"Where's Austin?"

"He had practice for the Christmas pageant after school." Natalie followed her mother into the apartment's tiny galley kitchen. "The final performance is next week. Remember I told you about it? I know Austin would love it if you came to the show."

"Bring him by The Tavern," Trudy answered. "Some of the regulars would get a kick out of him singing the songs."

Natalie fought the urge to grind her teeth. "He's not going to do a one-man show at the bar, Mom."

"No need for that uppity tone. You spent plenty of time there as a kid, and you turned out just fine."

Just fine. Right.

"I brought you some groceries to get you through the next few days. They're predicting six inches overnight." She took the bag off her shoulder and sat it on the counter.

"That isn't a grocery bag." Her mom pointed to the cloth sack.

"It's a reusable bag, Mom." This was one more of Trudy's quirks. Not only was her mother particular about what she bought, she didn't like her groceries to come from any other store than the one she favored. "I went to Safeway, the one you like close to town."

"I like to have those plastic bags," Trudy said, still eyeing the deep purple sack as if it was a snake about to strike. "I use them for lots of things around the house."

Natalie stalked over to the kitchen sink and threw open the cabinet door. An avalanche of white plastic grocery bags tumbled out. "You're covered," she snapped, then immediately felt guilty as her mother's face fell.

"I didn't realize I had so many," Trudy muttered, worrying her fingers together. "I like to have them around the house."

"It's okay." Natalie stepped forward to give her mother a short hug. Trudy might drive her crazy with her fears and routines, but Natalie couldn't imagine what it was like to actually live inside her mother's mind all the time. "Let's just unpack the food, okay?"

She'd bought the frozen dinners and cereal her mother preferred and two boxes of microwave popcorn. She'd also purchased a small bag of baby carrots and a carton of blueberries. She knew they'd probably turn to slime in the fridge—her mother wasn't one for fresh fruits or vegetables. But in the same way she introduced Austin to healthy foods, Natalie kept trying.

"Mom, we're having Christmas at Ruth's farmhouse this year," she said as she moved cans of diet soda out of the way to make room on a front shelf in the refrigerator for the blueberries. "Austin would love it if you were there with us. He's officially too old for Santa Claus, but that won't stop him from waking at the crack of dawn to open presents." She put the frozen dinners away, then turned to her mother. "You could spend the night Christmas Eve. There's room."

Before Natalie had finished the sentence, Trudy shook her head. "I'm working both nights. Can't do it." She took the boxes of popcorn and added them to the supply in her small pantry.

"It's crazy that The Tavern stays open on Christmas." Natalie couldn't help the bitterness that crept into her voice. "You've been working holidays there since I can remember. You can get one year off."

"I don't mind. Lots of locals look forward to a break over the holidays and stop in for a drink. Most of the other girls working there have families they need to see."

"Hello, you have a family."

Trudy rearranged the popcorn boxes until the way they were stacked met her arbitrary standards. "Brad called again yesterday. He told me he tried to reach you. You've got to answer, Natalie. Talk to him."

"So he can ask me for more money? No, thanks." She folded the reusable grocery bag and tucked it under her arm.

"He wants to come home, sweetie. Give him a chance. Your dad certainly never entertained the idea of coming to Crimson to be with us."

Natalie had always blamed her father for letting Trudy leave, felt as if she and her mother weren't good enough to hold his love and attention. That's what she'd been taught. Finally she realized that might not be the whole story.

"Did my father ask you to stay with him?"

Trudy's hand stilled on the door to the pantry, and she turned slowly. "You know things were hard for me in Atlanta. I was alone, had no family. He worked all the time. I needed to come home. If he loved me, he would have understood that, respected my decision."

It wasn't a direct answer, but it was enough of an admission to send the narrative Natalie had allowed to define her life down a different path. There'd been more to the story than the neglected young wife, with only her baby to love. She'd clung to the idea that her mother had returned to Crimson because she wanted to protect Natalie from the dangers of the big city and a father who would put her safety in jeopardy. There was a fine line between a safe haven and a cage.

"Did he ever want to see me?"

Her mother barked out a laugh. "As if I would let him take you away from here."

The shift from her identity as a child rejected by one parent to one held prisoner by the other split through Natalie, a crack in the ice around her heart.

"Is he still in Atlanta? Do you know?"

"He stopped calling years ago," her mother said with a dismissive sniff. "Once I convinced him that you weren't going to leave Crimson and—"

"I was going to leave." Natalie's heart began pounding against her rib cage and she took a breath to control the anxiety that bubbled to the surface. "For college. I was going to leave with Liam."

"But you didn't. You were meant to stay here, just like me."

A voice roared inside Natalie. *No. Nothing like you.*

Trudy glanced out the small window above the sink. "It's getting bad out there. You'd better go before the roads are any worse."

Natalie nodded numbly, allowed her mother to wrap her in a hug, didn't flinch when Trudy whispered, "Give Brad a chance. If he comes back to Crimson, everything will work out."

She walked out of her mother's apartment, stood for a long time next to her car in the parking lot. Snow fell in fat flakes around her, blanketing everything with white. Her head tipped to the sky, the snow covered her face. She could almost hear the sizzle as the icy flakes hit her overheated skin. No matter how long she stood there, the burning inside her wouldn't ease. For years she'd made excuses for her mother's anxiety, minimized the impact of that legacy of fear on her own life.

It had cost her so much and it felt as if every single thing she'd lost, every experience she'd missed out on now flamed in her chest, demanding to be seen. She took off her coat, tossed it into the backseat of her car and rolled down all the windows as she drove across town to the farmhouse. Wind blew through the car and even when her teeth began to chatter and the tips of her fingers turned numb, she still felt feverish with regret and sorrow.

It was a struggle to make her fingers work the key in the ignition to turn off the car when she got to the farmhouse. She still didn't register the cold, but her hands were bright pink, her shoulders shivering violently.

Pull it together, she told herself, standing in the middle of the driveway. *You don't have time for a nervous breakdown.*

Austin would be home soon, and there was dinner to make, homework to oversee. Single mothers didn't get a night off. She took deep breaths, flexed and tightened her hands to help the circulation. She couldn't quite regain her self-control, and as she entered the house the shivering turned into full-blown, body-racking shakes.

Liam's SUV was in the driveway, and she wasn't sure what she wanted more—to wrap herself around him or run and hide so he didn't see her like this. Maybe she could make it up to her bedroom, shower and change quickly before Ruth or Liam noticed what a hot mess she was.

Of course, Ruth was waiting in the entry as she opened the front door.

"What were you doing without a coat in the snow?" the older woman asked, leaning on her cane. "You were like a statue in the driveway for at least five minutes."

"Dro-opped my ke-eys," Natalie managed through her chattering teeth. It was hard to make her jaw move to form the words.

"You're practically frozen solid." Ruth reached out a hand, her papery skin scratchy against Natalie's cheek. "Liam, we need you," she called, turning her head toward the main part of the house.

"I don't need—"

He was there a moment later, took one look at her and let out a string of curses. "What the hell happened to you?" He wore one of Ruth's old aprons around his neck. This one said I Licked the Bowl.

"Ni-ice a-pron." She tried to smile, but it hurt too much. As feeling returned to her body, every part of it felt as if she was being stabbed with pins and needles.

"Did you walk from your mother's?" Ruth asked, shaking her head.

"Caa-ar windows op-en. Ne-eded fresh a-air."

He grabbed her hands, lifting them to the light. "You're lucky you didn't get real frostbite. We need to warm you, get you out of those wet clothes."

"Aus-tin coming ho-ome."

"I can be here with Austin," Ruth said. "Take care of her, Liam."

She was having trouble concentrating on their words over the intense throbbing in her hands and feet. "Austin," she repeated.

"You don't want him to see you like this," Liam said softly. He scooped her into his arms and started up the stairs. She burrowed against him, her head in the crook of his neck as though she was a newborn snuggling into her mother for comfort. That's how she felt, exposed and raw, blinking in the bright light after being nestled in her cocoon of ignorance for so many years.

He cursed again. "Your hair is icy."

"It's co-old out-s-side."

"So why were you standing out in the snow? Driving with the windows down like it's the middle of summer?"

She didn't answer, only pressed her nose into the base of his throat.

He hissed out a breath but pulled her closer against him. Once inside the guest bedroom she used, he set her down on the edge of the bed. She wanted to protest, to beg him to not let her go. But that would be too pathetic, even in a moment when almost every ounce of her pride had been torn to shreds.

Natalie didn't break down. No matter what life threw at her, she kept going, moving forward.

Until now.

"Can you get undressed?" he asked, then took hold of her hands again, frowning as he squeezed them carefully. "Never mind."

She tucked them under her legs as he disappeared into the bathroom connected to her bedroom. A moment later the sound of running water broke the silence of the room. Normally, Natalie would be embarrassed at the thought of Liam preparing a bath for her, but all she could feel now was anticipation of the warm water. Where her body had burned after her conversation with her mother, it was now icy cold.

A sliver of pride made its way to the surface and she tried to undo the buttons of her denim shirt. Surely she didn't need Liam for every part of this experience. But her clumsy, still-frozen fingers fumbled on the buttons.

"Let me," he said, returning to her.

Her gaze flicked away, mortified as he stripped her with efficient movements, so different from the way he'd taken off her clothes at other times. She stood, pushing down her wet yoga pants, goose bumps rising on her skin. He held out her flannel robe and she slipped her arms in, grateful for the warmth. More grateful as he led her to the bath and the steam in the small room seeped into her pores. He'd added bubbles to the water, the smell of lavender filled the air.

She breathed it in, letting the familiar scent melt away some of her shame. "I can ha-andle it fro-om here."

He didn't move, only stood in the doorway with arms shoved into the pockets of his jeans. His eyes were dark and gentle, as if he knew better than she did what had motivated her recklessness today.

"Fine," she muttered, her need to step into the bath overcoming her reluctance to do so in front of him. As soon as her toes hit the water, she cringed and drew back.

"It's going to hurt at first," Liam offered.

"You think?" She took a fortifying breath and plunged one foot, then the other, into the water. Maybe it was good that he was watching. It made her move more quickly than she would have otherwise. She lowered herself into the tub until she was submerged to her shoulders, biting back a groan of pain as the warm water brought life back into her fingers.

He pushed off from the door, and she covered her breasts—an unconscious response. One side of his mouth curved but he walked past the tub, flipped down the lid on the toilet and sat. "Don't worry," he said, humor lacing his tone. "I'll let you defrost fully before I make my big move."

"I didn't mean..." she started, then paused, thinking of all the places she could go with that sentence. "Thank you for taking care of me." She tipped back her head to look at him, offered a small smile to let him know she was okay.

He pulled off the sweater he wore and folded it on his lap. The white T-shirt underneath revealed his wide shoulders and the muscles in his arms. His skin glistened a little from the steam. Natalie realized he was still the most beautiful man she'd ever seen. "You're welcome."

They sat together in a silence more companionable than awkward. Natalie felt her equilibrium—some sense of it—returning. There was so much she wanted to say but was afraid if she tried now the words would get jumbled and she'd make a mess of it, the way she had with so many things involving this man.

When Liam had shown up in Crimson years ago, she'd pinned all her hopes on him. He was like a shiny penny, "Calgon, take me away," and her deepest, secret desires all rolled into one slightly aloof and slightly belligerent package. She hated to admit it, but she'd wanted him to rescue her, whisk her away to a happy-ever-after future—the details of which always stayed slightly out of focus.

The accident that killed Beth Travers changed him, made him sharper and no longer such a safe bet. Natalie hadn't been able to see him through that. She hadn't been brave enough to share her fears, so they'd grown and multiplied until they ruined the two of them.

"I'm sorry," she whispered when the bubbles began to evaporate. Using the toe of one foot, she turned the faucet knob to add more hot water to the bath.

"Don't apologize for being human." Liam bent next to the bathtub, using one finger to peel a strand of wet hair away from her cheek and tuck it behind her ear. "It happens to the best of us." He tipped up her chin so she would look at him, his gaze holding none of the judgment she felt she deserved.

She nodded, gratitude for his understanding unfurling like a blanket inside of her. Natalie had always forced herself to be strong in front of other people, even her closest friends. If she showed them her weaknesses, exposed her fears, they might think she was like her mother. Liam had seen the worst in her tonight, but he didn't seem bothered by it the way she expected.

"Do you want to talk about what happened with your mom?"

She shook her head, relieved when Liam didn't argue.

"I'm going to check on Ruth and Austin, then finish dinner. Do you feel up to joining us?"

"I'll be down in a few minutes."

He pressed a gentle kiss to her mouth and left, leaving her with only the sound of the water as she leaned forward, stretched her tight muscles. As quickly as the emotional upheaval had started, it was over. She was finished, ready to return to real life. She needed the familiar pattern of routine to fully right her.

So she climbed out, drained the bath and got dressed. She couldn't manage more than her coziest pajamas but didn't figure anyone in the house would care. As soon as she walked down the steps and saw Austin at the kitchen table, bent over his homework, she returned fully to herself. The problems were still there—her mother's increasingly erratic behavior, her scumbag ex-husband, decades of decisions based on unfounded fear. But she had her son, and she would wade through the rest to make sure he had the life he deserved.

Her steps faltered as Liam, unaware she was there, came up behind Austin, put his hand on the boy's shoulders and leaned forward to explain a math problem to him. The breath got caught in her throat as her heart beat out a message that said, *Yes, that. Right there. Our future is right there.*

She didn't bother to deny it. The only question was how to make sure it would happen.

Chapter Fourteen

Liam blew out a relieved breath when Natalie finally came down the steps. She'd scared the hell out of him earlier.

He understood that she was overdue for losing it a little and guessed it had been years in the making. A person could only hold themselves that tight for so long before the coil of their life became razor thin then snapped.

What surprised him was that he wanted to be there during the break, to support her however she needed him to until she was back on two feet again and even after. The normalcy of making dinner, even pasta and store-bought sauce, of helping Austin with his homework, soothed the restless part of Liam. Usually when things got tough, he took off and let Tanner do the cleanup. He'd start another venture, set up meetings, meet so-called friends in far-flung vacation destinations—anything to keep himself from getting in too deep.

But that need to move on had shifted, which was part

of the reason that where LifeMap was headquartered had become so important to him. For the first time in his life, Liam wanted a home base. He hadn't really considered Crimson as a candidate for that base. There were too many emotional land mines for him in this town. But tonight made him rethink that in a serious way. He liked being the person Natalie leaned on, the man who could be someone else's true north. He wanted to be that guy and she finally seemed willing to let him try.

After dinner, he texted Tanner to schedule another meeting with the town council. The next couple of days he spent with Jase, touring the area with a commercial Realtor, meeting with local business owners and representatives from the school district. He had to admit the town did its best to roll out the red carpet and made a good case for why Crimson would be the right fit for LifeMap.

Liam had all but signed on the dotted line in Vermont, so he quickly put those plans on hold until he could determine what he wanted for his future. Whatever it was, he was certain it involved Natalie.

Several times in the days following her afternoon in the snow, she'd started to open up to him, but something always stopped her. He wished he knew what it was, why she couldn't quite trust him enough. He wondered if it would make a difference if he shared his doubts about staying in Crimson. Had people in town truly forgotten about his past here, or were they just willing to overlook it because of the potential LifeMap had to help the local economy? He hated the legacy of abandonment he'd inherited from his parents. It was hard for him to believe that he wouldn't be rejected by anyone, any place that mattered to him, which made the thought of staying in town all the more daunting.

As he drove Natalie and Austin toward downtown

and the winter carnival Saturday morning, she reached across the front seat and took his hand in hers, rubbing her thumb across his knuckles. Austin sat in the backseat with his headphones on, oblivious to anything but the game he was playing on his iPad.

"Thank you for coming in early with me to help set up." Natalie rolled her head along the back of the seat and smiled at him.

"I'm happy to be with you." He lifted her hand to his mouth and pressed a kiss to the inside of her wrist. "Olivia told me that the arts and crafts fair is juried. You had to submit pieces and be selected by the Winterfest board. That's quite an accomplishment."

She dismissed the compliment with a wave of her hand. "Olivia is on the board so that helps."

"I've seen how hard you work, Nat. Your jewelry is exceptionally crafted. You should own your talent."

She tugged at her hand, making him smile. Things were never easy with Natalie, which made it feel like an even bigger accomplishment when she let him in.

"I'm trying," she said after a moment. "Being in the art fair is the first step. It's the first time I've sold my own pieces, been in front of potential customers. Normally I give everything to Olivia to sell at the gift shop that's part of the community center. I like the anonymity." She took a shuddering breath. "What if everyone walks right by me today?"

"Not going to happen," he answered immediately.

"You sound so sure," she whispered.

"I'm sure of you."

Biting down on her lip, she turned her head to look out the window of the SUV. "Liam, I need to tell you…" She paused, cleared her throat. "I want you to understand…"

Now she did pull her hand away, tucked both of hers between her knees.

"What, Natalie? What do you want me to understand?" He gripped the steering wheel as he waited for her answer.

The rosy pink of her lip turned white as she sunk her teeth into it. "I want you to know, know…how much I appreciate your support," she said on a rush of breath.

No. Let me in, he wanted to roar.

"Of course, sweetheart." He glanced at her out of the corner of his eye. "That's what I'm here for."

She turned to look at him. Her face was flushed, her dark eyes shining. Suddenly it didn't matter how much she was holding back. He was willing to take whatever emotions she would give him, even if they were scraps of the truth.

He parked the car on one of the side streets near the community center where the arts and crafts fair would be held. Winterfest was a full day of activities including ice sculptures, skating on the rink at the center of town and the craft fair. Then as the sun went down, everyone would gather for the lighting of the Crimson Christmas tree on the town square. Downtown was already full of festive holiday lights, but traditionally the huge Douglas fir designated as the official town tree was saved until right before before Christmas.

Because none of the activities had started, only volunteers and vendors filled the streets. He and Austin unloaded the trunk that held her jewelry out of the back of the SUV, while Natalie went ahead to check in with the art fair organizers. It was hard to believe that all the time and energy she'd put in over the past few weeks could fit into one medium-size suitcase. Then again, jewelry was small and light. She also had display stands and things to decorate her table. As they walked toward the community center, a number of people waved hello and several stopped them to talk. The community center's main room was filled with rows of tables.

He expected a barrage of questions about his plans for LifeMap but was asked about Ruth and his plans for Christmas instead. He saw Jase and another man he remembered from high school, Noah Crawford, who invited him to go backcountry skiing outside of Aspen over New Year's weekend. He told them he'd check his calendar but realized it was something he'd like to do. Other than Tanner, he didn't have anyone he'd consider a real friend. Again the inability to let anyone get too close had caused him to keep the people he met at arm's length. It was about time for that to change.

"I see Mom," Austin said, running ahead.

Natalie was in the aisle, talking to a younger guy who stood behind a nearby table filled with bowls carved out of wood. He leaned forward, touched her on the arm. She smiled, and Liam had a sudden urge to buy every ugly bowl on the table just so Natalie didn't spend the day next to another man.

"Looks good in here," he said, walking up to her and planting a kiss on her mouth.

Her eyes widened and she pulled back, glancing at Austin who was engrossed in the stained glass kaleidoscopes being sold by the vendor across the aisle from Natalie. The man she'd been talking to backed away, rearranging his display before beginning a conversation with the artist stationed next to him on the other side.

Natalie gave Liam's chest a gentle poke through his down coat. "I think you just marked me."

"Maybe," he admitted. "Does that bother you?"

Pink colored her cheeks and her mouth curved into a smile. "It's weird, but I kind of like it."

"I like you." He bent and kissed her again, this one more a pledge than a possession. *Coward*, a voice inside said. *Tell her you love her.* Later, he thought. Maybe tonight. The idea of saying the words out loud made his breath hitch. "Let's get you set up now. I want to make sure there's nothing else you need before the fair starts."

"I can handle things in here if you want to walk around or visit any businesses. I'm sure you've got more important things to do than be my assistant for the morning."

"All day," he clarified. "I'm your official assistant as long as you need me today. This is where I want to be, Nat. I promise."

True to his word, Liam stayed by her side as the art fair portion of Winterfest opened. It was a beautiful day, cold but clear with the bluebird sky famous in the mountains of Colorado. That helped the event to draw in crowds of shoppers, many looking to finish their last-minute Christmas shopping.

Natalie had a steady stream of people at her booth. Not just her friends as she'd expected, although Olivia and Millie stopped by and Katie gave out muffins to everyone around Natalie's table. Two women who'd driven over from Aspen sought her out. They told her they'd bought her bracelets from the gift shop the year before and gotten so many compliments on them where they lived in Dallas that they came to the show specifically to meet her. One of the women handed her a card and said she owned a boutique in the trendy Uptown neighborhood of Dallas and would love to carry a selection of Natalie's pieces in her store.

Natalie was so blown away she didn't know how to

answer, which is where Liam came in handy. He easily steered the conversation to customer base, timelines and a potential first order. He took the woman's card, tucked it in the pocket of Natalie's jeans as the women walked away.

"Good thing one of us knows something about the business end of this." She slipped her hand into her pocket, feeling the smooth edge of the card, wondering if her luck could really be turning around. If she grew her jewelry business, she could pay off her debt more quickly and start saving again. A concept that made happy tears prick at the back of her eyes.

"I need to stay useful so you'll keep me around." Liam said the words lightly, but there was something in his voice that made her wonder if he really believed that. Although he didn't talk about it, she knew how much it must have hurt to have his parents ship him off when he'd gotten too wild. She couldn't imagine sending Austin away, no matter what twists and turns his behavior took.

"Mom, I'm hungry." As if she'd summoned him, her son came to stand at her side.

"I love you, sweetie," she said, wrapping her arms around him.

He squirmed away like the boy he was. "I know, Mom. Can you give me money for lunch? They've got food trucks set up around the square."

Natalie hesitated, glancing up and down the aisle to look for one of her friends. "Let me find someone to walk with you." Her mother's comments about Brad coming back to town echoed in her mind. Not that she expected her ex-husband to do something funny with Austin, but she wasn't going to take any chances.

"I'll go with him." Liam glanced up from his phone. Tanner had stopped by the booth a half hour earlier and told Liam there were some emails he'd forwarded that needed responses right away. Natalie expected Liam to use work as an excuse to leave, but he'd pulled up a chair and stayed with her instead.

"It's okay," she said automatically. "I know you have work."

"The emails will wait." He stood, ruffling Austin's hair. "Let's get some food. We'll bring something back for your mom, too."

Austin nodded, as if it was perfectly normal. "The Mexican restaurant has a food truck. She likes tacos."

Liam glanced at Natalie. "Tacos sound good?"

All she could do was smile and nod, then watch them walk away. It was silly, she knew, but the idea that she wasn't alone, didn't have to handle everything, even for one day, was overwhelming in its relief.

"Your husband is a good dad."

Startled, she glanced at the older couple standing in front of her table. Arms linked, the woman studied her jewelry while the man looked at Natalie.

"He's not," she stammered. "That isn't my husband."

The man shrugged, almost reluctantly letting go of his wife's hand as she held a pair of earrings up to the light. "Well, you can tell he cares about the boy. We raised four sons."

"Heaven help me," the woman muttered.

"They were a handful," the man agreed. "But all of them turned out okay."

"Because they had you as a role model," his wife added. She held out the earrings to Natalie. "I'm going to get these for my daughter-in-law. She's pregnant with our first grandbaby."

"Congratulations," Natalie said, clearing her throat

when her voice caught. She rang up the purchase, wrapped the earrings and watched the couple walk away.

Austin needed more good men in his life. Her friends' husbands were there for support, but it wasn't enough. She'd tried to be everything for her son, but there were just some things she couldn't manage. The fact that Liam seemed both willing to step into the role and so natural at it made her heart expand even more.

The rest of the day passed in a blur of friendship and activity. The crowd at the craft fair waned over lunch then surged again in the early afternoon. An hour before the fair was set to close, Natalie sold her last bracelet.

All her friends had stopped by, which almost made up for the fact that her mother hadn't come to see her. She hadn't really expected it. Trudy hated crowds, especially when they were filled with tourists and nonlocals. But hope was like an early spring crocus high in the mountains, blooming at the first sign of warmth and sunlight only to be buried by another snowfall.

Would she ever stop wanting her mom's approval? This was one more lesson she tucked away in her imaginary mother's playbook. She would make sure Austin never doubted her love and pride in him for whatever path he took. Even if it left her shaking with fear, she would support him. Even if it meant overcoming her own fear and heading to the ocean so he could ride the waves and feel the sand between his toes.

She'd made close to a thousand dollars today. Instead of using the money for her debts, she was going to look for plane tickets someplace warm for spring break. The thought made her giddy with nerves and excitement.

After packing up, she went to check out the other Winterfest activities with Liam and Austin. They skated, had hot chocolate with extra marshmallows, watched the ice sculptures being carved, then met up with her friends and Tanner for dinner at the brewery that had opened just a few weeks ago in the center of town.

They headed back to the square for the lighting of the Christmas tree and joined in as Jase and other members of the town council led the crowd in several carols. The sun had set, the sky inky above the glowing lights of the town. Natalie couldn't remember when she'd had a happier day.

As the festival drew to a close, the group decided to go back to the brewery. From habit, Natalie pulled away. "I'm going to take Austin home," she told Liam, who stood talking to his assistant. "It's been a long day for him and I want to check on Ruth. The nurse with her texted that everything is fine, but I should still get back."

"I'll take him," Tanner offered immediately. "You need to celebrate that sellout at the fair."

"That's nice but—"

"It's okay, Mom." Austin took a step toward Tanner. "I'm going to show him how to spawn dogs and build a shelter on 'Minecraft.'"

"I understand about half of what you just said," she told her son with a smile. "But I'm pretty sure Tanner doesn't play 'Minecraft.'"

Liam coughed, but it sounded more like a laugh.

Tanner narrowed his eyes at Liam before turning to Natalie. "I have twelve diamond swords."

"Which is good?"

"Very good," Austin confirmed.

"It's how I unwind," Tanner said with an unapologetic shrug. "You should also know I have five younger brothers and sisters, and my grandmother lived with us for the last three years of her life. I can handle this."

Liam nodded. "Tanner can handle anything."

"If you're sure," Natalie agreed after a moment. "Austin, you need to listen to Tanner and bedtime is nine thirty."

"Mom," Tanner said on a whine. "It's the weekend."

"Nine thirty," she repeated. "Tanner, call me if Ruth needs anything."

Tanner put his arm around the boy's shoulders. "We've got this."

"When he was a toddler," Natalie murmured as they walked away, "he had separation anxiety so bad he'd scream every time I left him at day care. I couldn't go to the bathroom on the weekend without him crying out-side the door."

"That must have been difficult."

"Not as hard as watching him walk away without me."

He laced his fingers with hers. "One beer. I'll have you home in time to kiss him good-night."

"Are you sure?" She let him begin to lead her down the sidewalk toward the brewery. The rest of her friends had already disappeared inside. "If you want to stay later—"

"I want to be wherever you are." He tugged her into the shadows of a storefront doorstep and kissed her, claimed her.

When he finally let her go, she didn't step away. Her arms wound around his neck and she nipped at his bottom lip, deepening the kiss as he sucked in a breath, claim-ing him right back.

Chapter Fifteen

By the time they entered the brewery, Liam had counted backward from one hundred, composed several work-related emails in his head and, as a last-ditch effort to calm down, thought of his third-grade teacher in her underwear. It was barely enough to allow some of the blood that had pooled south of his head to return to his brain.

No other way to describe it, Natalie had kissed him senseless. He loved it, loved her. The buzz he felt had nothing to do with the beer he'd had earlier. They joined Natalie's friends—his friends—at a grouping of high-top tables in front of the bar.

Everyone cheered for Natalie, but Liam got the real thrill as she clasped more tightly to his hand. In front of her friends. As if they were together. For real.

This was it. His real life, the life he'd never known he wanted.

It was normal in a way Liam had dismissed for the past ten years. He'd been so busy helping his father build an empire, then working harder to break free from that empire. He'd traveled, partied, worked around the clock. Whatever he thought it would take to outrun the voices in his head. The ones that told him no matter how much money and power he had, he wasn't good enough. But in Crimson, with its quaint charm and everyday activities, he felt at peace.

"You a Broncos fan?" Noah Crawford asked.

"Giants." Liam took a pull from his beer.

"I won't hold that against you."

Liam laughed and they talked football and Super Bowl predictions.

Noah grabbed hold of Katie as she walked by, looping his arm around her neck and scrubbing her head with his knuckles, big brother–style. Liam saw her cringe against the contact, but Noah didn't seem to notice. "Katie doesn't miss a game. And she makes the best blue-and-orange cookies for Sundays during the season. Don't sell any to this guy, Bug. He's a Giants fan."

Katie pulled herself out of his grasp. "Liam is one of my new favorite customers. He doesn't call me annoying nicknames that I grew out of years ago."

"I appreciate that," Liam said, and she gave him a grateful smile.

"But I'm your all-time favorite, right? Even with the nickname?" Noah chucked her on the shoulder and her smile went tight.

"How long are you in town, Noah?" she asked.

"Probably through New Year's. My mom is upset that Emily is staying on the East Coast for the holidays." He turned to Liam. "My sister married Thomas Whitaker last year. You know any of them?"

Liam gave a low whistle under his breath. "I think everyone knows the Whitakers." They were an old-school political dynasty family from Connecticut, a version of the Kennedys with less tragedy and scandal. "I've met Thomas a few times. He's the second-oldest brother?"

Noah nodded. "He's got the same political ambitions as his father. Who knows, my sister could end up First Lady some day."

"Is she happy?" Katie asked suddenly.

"She's living the dream. Of course she's happy." Noah looked confused by the question. Liam would have felt that same way a few weeks ago, but now he understood what she meant.

Sara called Katie over to where the women stood at the corner of the bar, and she seemed relieved for an excuse to walk away from Noah.

"Did you two date at some point?" Liam asked when she'd gone.

Noah laughed, almost choking on his beer. "Katie and me? Are you kidding? No way."

"Right. She's gorgeous, fun, apparently loves football and is an incredible baker. I can see why she wouldn't hold any appeal."

Noah looked almost surprised by Liam's description of the bakery owner. "It's not that she isn't appealing. Katie and I have been buds since high school. I dated her best friend back then and Katie was just…Katie. I don't think of her like that."

"Well, someone's bound to," Liam said with a shrug. "Whoever it is will be a lucky guy."

"Sure," Noah agreed absently. "A lucky guy for sure."

Logan and Josh joined them and the conversation turned to ski conditions in Aspen and the renovation project Logan was finishing. Liam thought about asking him to look at the farmhouse. Since Ruth wanted to stay there, he'd make sure it was state-of-the-art and accessible for all her needs as her health inevitably deteriorated. They'd given up her room at the assisted living center because she was more determined than ever to live in her own house.

Ruth had always been a master at getting what she wanted. His gaze caught on Natalie and he wondered with a start how much of the circumstances of his return to Crimson had been orchestrated by his former nanny. For all he knew, the disappearance of the money had been her way of ensuring he'd come to town to check things out. He certainly wouldn't put it past her.

Natalie glanced at her watch then over to him. He said goodbye to the group and they headed out, holding hands as they walked through the quiet streets to his SUV. Again, the normalcy of the moment made his heart surge. This is what had been missing in his life. Normal.

As he turned the key in the ignition, his phone began to ding. He dug it out of his pocket. Service could be spotty in some parts of town, and he quickly realized the increasingly urgent texts from Tanner had been coming in over the past half hour.

"Everything okay?" Natalie asked.

He read the messages, his gut tightening, then threw the car into gear. "We've got to get to the farmhouse now."

Natalie turned, suddenly alert. "What's the matter? Is it Ruth? Austin?"

"It's Brad Holt," he said as he took a sharp turn, fishtailing a little on the fresh dusting of snow that had fallen. "Your ex-husband picked tonight for his big return."

Natalie didn't wait for the SUV to come to a complete stop before she opened the door and ran toward the farmhouse. She heard Liam calling to her but kept moving forward. The image of Brad with Austin and her not in the picture had taken hold in her mind and wouldn't let go.

Liam had tried to talk to her on the short ride from downtown to the house, but she'd barely heard anything he'd said, couldn't process the reassurances. This was, to her mind, the worst of all possible scenarios. The house of cards she'd so carefully constructed tumbling down around her.

Tanner opened the front door just as she came up the porch steps. "Everything's under control," he said, his voice soothing. "A completely normal visit."

Natalie pushed passed him and headed for the main living area. Nothing about her ex-husband showing up right before Christmas was normal. Her mother must have told him Liam was in town and that she'd seen Natalie with him. The thought of an easy mark would motivate Brad more than anything else.

She stopped short when she saw Brad, Austin and Ruth seated around the kitchen table, each holding a hand of cards. Brad was still handsome in that rangy way he had, but he looked pale, his eyes shifting back and forth nervously between Austin and Ruth. Blood roared through Natalie's head as she charged forward.

"What do you think you're doing?" Without thinking she slapped her ex-husband's cards onto the table. "He's nine, Brad. Too early for poker or blackjack or whatever else you're teaching."

"Mom!" Austin yelled her name, and she turned. His eyes were wide with shock, twin spots of color bright on his cheeks. "I was showing him how to play crazy eights."

Silence crackled in the room like the flames of a bonfire. It was clear Austin was waiting for her to explain herself, why she was acting like a lunatic in front of a father he'd seen only a handful of times in the past five years. How to explain that she was trying to protect him? Could a child understand that sometimes the greatest danger came from people you wanted to love the most?

"Sorry, bud," she whispered. "I...I didn't realize."

Ruth set a gentle hand on her arm. "You and Austin are safe here. Always." She glanced at Brad, narrowed her eyes. "From any threat."

"What are you talking about, Miss Ruth?" Austin carefully placed his cards on the table, facedown as if they would resume the game once things got worked out. "My dad is here to visit for Christmas. He brought me a gift." His eyes strayed to an unwrapped package on the counter. A Thomas & Friends backpack. Natalie sighed. Austin hadn't been interested in trains since preschool, which was probably the last time Brad had spent any time with the boy.

Ruth opened her mouth, glanced at Natalie.

"Austin, it's almost ten. Way past your bedtime," Natalie said.

"No," the boy whined. "Dad is here. You can't make me go to bed, Mom. He's my parent, too. Doesn't he get a say?"

She clamped her hand to her stomach. Those words sliced her open.

"Lighten up, Nat. It's the holidays. Don't be a grinch." She felt the menace of Brad's smile, a silent acknowledgment of the subtle shifting of power. She knew he would exploit it to his advantage.

Before she could argue, Liam stepped forward from where he and Tanner stood at the edge of the room. "Austin, you heard your mother." They all turned at the tone of command in Liam's voice. She'd seen him angry, laughing, passionate. A full range of emotions. But this was different, powerful and commanding. As he stood there it was easy to see him as the head of his company, a captain of industry, in charge of all he could see. And he was using that power to support her. It took her breath away.

Dragging his feet but unable to disobey, Austin pushed back from the table. At the same time Brad turned, pointed a finger at Liam. "This doesn't concern you, Donovan."

"It does now," Liam answered, unmoved.

"It's okay, Dad," Austin said quickly. "I'm kind of tired. But I'll see you tomorrow, right? You're staying in town through Christmas?"

"You bet." Brad threw a glare in Natalie's direction. "I've got things to keep me busy in town. We can spend lots of QT together."

"Will you come to my Christmas pageant?"

"Wouldn't miss it."

The hope in Austin's face made Natalie want to cry. She knew that hope, lived with it for years. It had broken her heart more times than she could count. She didn't want that for her son. There had been so many things given up for the sake of keeping Austin safe. How could it be wrecked so easily?

Liam stepped behind her, his hand warm on her back just when she was about to lunge at her ex-husband. "Not worth it," he whispered into her ear. "Not in front of Austin, anyway."

She closed her hand into a fist, her fingernails digging into the fleshy pad of her palm as she tried to regain control of her emotions. "I'll make sure your dad gets the details for the pageant," she told Austin. "But now it really is bedtime."

"I'll walk him up," Tanner volunteered. "I still have 'Minecraft' questions for you." He pointed a finger at Austin.

The boy gave Ruth a kiss and hug, fist-bumped Liam

and hugged Natalie. She breathed in the scent of him, so familiar and precious to her. He took a step toward the hallway, then turned to his father, clearly unsure of how to say good-night to a parent he barely knew.

In the end, Brad stuck out his hand and Austin awkwardly shook it. "'Night, sport."

Austin looked uncertain whether he liked the unfamiliar nickname. Then he smiled shyly. "'Night, Dad."

"Don't do this," Natalie said on an angry hiss of breath when she heard Austin pounding up the stairs. "You're going to break his heart, Brad."

"How do you figure, Nat?" Brad flicked a glance at Liam then Ruth. "Got anything better than water to drink around here?"

"Not for you," Ruth said, crossing her arms over her chest.

"He loves you." Natalie threw her arms wide. "You haven't done a damn thing for him his whole life and he loves you. When you take off without a word, it's going to hurt him. The last time you swept into his life was different. He was younger and he doesn't remember much. Now he knows. He understands the rejection on a different level."

"Spare me the pyschobabble." Brad sank back into the chair. "Just because you and your mom are nut jobs—"

"Enough." Liam moved to stand directly in front of Brad's chair. "I don't know what point you were trying to make here tonight, but the show's over. You need to leave. Now."

Brad shook his head. "My wife and I have some unfinished business."

"Ex-wife."

"I've got nothing to say to you, Brad."

"We'll always be connected, Nat. Don't try to deny it. If you want to keep my son tucked away in this little world you've created for him, there's a price. Otherwise, it would be my pleasure to introduce him to the world beyond these mountains."

"I said get out." Liam reached for Brad, who jumped out of the chair, sending it flying, and gave Liam a hard shove. Tanner rushed back into the room, but Natalie held up a hand before he intervened. She was going to handle her ex-husband this time.

She stepped between Liam and Brad before either could take a swing. Pressing her hand against the hard wall of Liam's chest, she felt his heart beating. "Not worth it," she said, repeating his words from earlier. Then she faced her ex-husband. "Brad—"

"I'm not going to let him order me around, Nat. If he wants—"

"Ten thousand." Ruth's voice rang out, a slight tremble to it, making all three of them turn.

She pointed a bony finger at Brad. "Another ten thousand dollars and you leave town tomorrow morning, after saying goodbye to Austin. For good, this time."

Natalie felt Liam step away, leaving her holding on to air. Her hand dropped along with her heart. "No," she whispered. "Not this. Not now."

Chapter Sixteen

"Now we're talking, old lady. I knew you'd come through again eventually."

Liam was still trying to process Ruth's words when Brad made the comment. All the self-control he'd held on to since walking into the house shattered. He pushed Natalie out of the way and swung, leveling his fist into her ex-husband's face with a satisfying thunk.

Brad stumbled back, then came at him with a growl. Liam was momentarily distracted when Natalie got shoved to the ground in the process. Distracted long enough for Brad to land a punch before tackling Liam to the ground. He heard something break and Ruth's scream, and then Brad was lifted off him.

He scrambled to his feet, ready to go again, but Tanner held the other man tight. Brad struggled, and Tanner gripped him harder, twisting Brad's arms behind his back. Liam hadn't been joking when he said Tanner could handle anything.

"*Another* ten thousand? This is where the money went?" He turned to Ruth. "You paid off her ex-husband?"

"You haven't heard the whole story, Liam." Ruth met his gaze without apology.

"And whose fault is that?" He looked at Natalie, who had gotten up off the floor as well and stood to one side of the table, her arms clenched to her sides. "You knew." The words were a statement, not a question.

She shook her head. "Not for sure." But her eyes flicked away from his, telling him more than her words.

"Dude, call off your bodyguard." Brad winced as Tanner jerked his arms. The skin around his eye was already bruising. He'd have a full-blown shiner by morning. The thought that he'd put the mark there gave Liam some perverse satisfaction, tempered as he ran a hand over his own throbbing jaw.

"Leave now, Brad." When Brad would have protested, Liam held up a hand. "One more word from you and I'll call the cops, and you can explain to them how you ended up with Ruth's money."

"She gave it to me," Brad protested. "She contacted me."

"Let him go," Liam told Tanner, stepping closer. "I'm going to be watching you. If you come anywhere near her again, I will destroy you. Ruth is no longer part of whatever is going on between you and Natalie. It's done."

Brad shook out his arms but backed away. "We're not finished," he yelled at Natalie, ignoring Liam. "If you want to keep me out of Austin's life so badly, you know what it will take. Maybe this well has run dry." He pointed to Ruth, and Liam wanted to rip the finger off his hand. "But you'll find another one, babe." He nodded toward Liam while continuing to stare at Natalie. "I know how resourceful you can be."

"Get out." Tanner pushed Brad toward the door, then followed him out of the room.

"I'll give you a call tomorrow, Nat. Tell Austin I'll see him real soon."

Needing something to do with his hands so he didn't wrap them around Brad's neck, Liam stalked to the kitchen. He took out a liquor bottle from the cabinet above the refrigerator, poured at least two shots' worth into a glass and downed it. The dark liquid burned his throat, making him hiss, but it didn't wash away the taste of blood and hate in his mouth.

All the things he hadn't understood over the past few weeks fell into place at the same time his life rocked on its axis. Why hadn't Natalie told him the situation with her ex-husband? He could have fixed it if he'd known. It killed him to think she still didn't trust him. When he turned, Natalie was kneeling beside Ruth.

"I'm so sorry," she whispered, tears streaming down her cheeks. "I didn't realize it was that much. You should never have been involved in any of this."

"It's fine, dearie." Ruth patted Natalie's head the same way she used to do to Liam when he was a boy.

"No." Both women turned to him as he spoke. He poured another drink, swallowed and came back to the kitchen table. "Nothing about this situation is fine. I'll be calling the director of Evergreen in the morning."

Natalie's face went ashen, her eyes wide and full of pain, guilt and disbelief.

Join the club, he thought.

"You will do no such thing." Suddenly Ruth was no longer pushing eighty years old. It was twenty years ago and she was saying the exact words, in the exact tone, she'd used when Liam was ten and told her his plan to run away from home. The thought that someone had taken advantage of this woman who'd cared for him as if he belonged to her made his gut clench. The idea that Natalie had stood by and allowed it to happen ripped his chest right open.

"She didn't know anything about me giving money to Brad," Ruth continued. "He's right, I contacted him. I *chose* to give him the money. You put it in my bank account, and I have a right to spend it however I want." She put a hand on Natalie's shoulder. "Someone had to protect her."

"Tell me how this happened," he said to Natalie. "The whole story."

She straightened before answering, as if refusing to be on her knees in front of him. Despite the fury that pounded through him, he admired her for that.

The explanation she gave him was long and complex, detailing the early days of her marriage to Brad traveling for work to the debt and manipulation that followed.

"Why did you marry him in the first place?" he interrupted at one point, unable to believe the woman he knew would commit herself to a guy like Brad Holt. Or maybe it was just his ego that needed soothing since she'd married Brad within a year of rejecting Liam.

"Because I had to get away from my mother, and marriage seemed like my best chance," she answered, no emotion in her tone. "I didn't particularly care who was standing on the other side of the aisle at that point. You'd left, breaking my heart in the process. I wasn't sure I'd ever be able to love someone again, so what did it matter?"

The vulnerability of what she revealed wrecked him. He'd cast himself as the wronged party in their breakup. She'd moved on with life, married another man. Now he saw it in a new light, that she'd run away just like he had, only she'd done it in a different way.

"You see, Liam?" Ruth said, wiping away tears. "I had to help her."

"No," Natalie said, her cheeks now dry. "This is my mess, and I shouldn't have confided in you, Ruth. Liam's right. You're my patient and I took advantage of that relationship."

Ruth huffed out a breath. "I was your friend before I hired you, and that never changed. You're a good girl. You work your fanny off and everyone knows it." She stood, giving Natalie a hug and whispering something in her ear that brought a ghost of a smile to Nat's pale face. Then she turned her attention to Liam. "What use is having money if I can't use it to help a friend in need?"

He pressed his lips together, reminding himself that wasn't the point. It would do no good to argue with Ruth.

She wrapped her thin arms around his middle. "You are the son I never had, Liam. I love you and it lit up my life to watch you grow. I appreciate how you take care of me now, and I'm glad you're back in Crimson, even if this mess is what brought you here. Don't throw away happiness because it doesn't come wrapped in a shiny package. Some of the best things in life have a little bite to them." She looked between the two of them. "This old lady's going to bed now. You two work things out. I hated watching you break apart ten years ago. It would be no different now."

Natalie nodded, but kept her eyes to the ground.

"I'll move out tomorrow morning," Natalie said into the silence that stretched between them as Ruth left the room.

"Why didn't you tell me?" His heart felt as though it was shrinking with every moment that passed. "Everything we shared over the past weeks didn't matter to you. You threw us away. Again."

Her eyes crashed into his, suddenly furious. "What exactly did I throw away, Liam? When were you planning to reveal that you'd practically committed to moving LifeMap to Vermont? You never planned to stay in Crimson. I was a detour on your path to more success, just like ten years ago."

"It wasn't a done deal," he muttered, but that wasn't the point, either. "I wanted a reason to change my mind, Natalie. I wanted you to be that reason."

She sighed and like a hole in a balloon, all the fight deflated out of her. It did no good to replay the last month over and over, to try to see a way she could have avoided this ending. It felt like her predetermined destiny. "I was never going to be the person you want me to be, Liam. It's like Ruth said, life is messy. I'm messy. I've got fears and troubles and it's what makes me who I am. I know who you are. You're the guy who walks away when things don't come easy." Kneeling once again, she began to pick up the pieces of the lamp that had fallen from an end table and shattered across the floor. "This was never going to be easy. So, yeah, I kept the secret. I should have told you that I suspected Ruth was involved in some way."

"Ten thousand dollars is a lot of ways, Nat."

She sat back on her heels, pointed a section of broken glass at him. "I swear I didn't know. I asked her, and when she denied it, I believed her. I wanted to believe her so I didn't push too hard. Just like you wanted to believe in me. We both learned a lesson. No Christmas miracles in Crimson this season. But I *will* pay her back, and I'll make sure Brad stays away from her. I'll stay away if that's what you want me to do."

"She won't let that happen." He blew out a breath. "She loves you and Austin too much."

"I know you want what's best for her."

"What's best is for me to leave town. Everyone was doing just fine before I came back."

No, she wanted to tell him.

Not me. I was dead inside and you brought me back to life.

Again.

But she didn't say those words, would not beg him to stay like she'd done a decade earlier. No one could fix the broken parts of her life, the ones that came from inside her. Not Liam with his confidence and power, not Ruth with her money. If Natalie was going to put her life on track, she needed to do it herself. Stop living in fear's shadow and step out into the light.

"What about your company?"

"You were right, Vermont is basically a done deal. Maybe I was willing to give Crimson a chance, but that isn't going to happen—"

"Because of me." She stood, throwing the larger pieces of glass into the trash can.

"Don't worry, Nat. I'll be the villain in the story, just like before. I'll leave and everyone in town can talk about how I led them on, gave them false hope." He paused, ran his fingers through his hair then added, "Then ran away. Apparently it's what I do."

"Liam—"

He held up a hand, cut her off. "I'll come by tomorrow to say goodbye to Ruth. I'd appreciate it if you weren't here when I did."

The words stung, but Natalie hid the hurt. She nodded, kept her voice even when she answered. "If that's what you want."

For just a moment she saw both pain and love swirling in his gray eyes, fighting to see which emotion would come out on top. Then he blinked, shuttering his gaze, and he was a blank canvas, a stranger in front of her despite all they'd shared. "You made what I want irrelevant with your lies," he said before walking away.

She stared after him, rooted to one spot on the floor. The ice in his words began to blanket her heart, freezing her emotions once more. The front door slammed and a minute later the headlights from his SUV shone through the window before disappearing again. He was gone.

And she was alone, with no one but herself to blame.

Chapter Seventeen

The town square was deserted the next morning when Liam parked at the curb. The sun hadn't yet risen and everything looked frozen and still in the predawn light. A few pieces of trash blew across the street in the icy wind. Another snowfall was on the way, he could smell it in the air. Definitely time to get out of town if he was starting to predict the weather with his nose. He had an app for that.

It was hard to imagine the happiness of last night now when his heart felt like a lead weight in his chest. In a few hours, downtown would be bustling again with last-minute shoppers and families out to enjoy the holiday spirit. Not Liam. His plan was to be gone by noon, heading back east where he could pretend to be living the life he wanted.

He pushed through the door to Jason Crenshaw's law office. Jase turned from where he stood behind the empty receptionist's desk and held up a pot of steaming coffee.

"Katie's bakery is about to open," he said with a smile. "You sure you don't want to head down there? I make terrible coffee."

"I'll take terrible." Liam pulled the knit cap off his head and stuffed it into his pocket. "I'm on a time crunch this morning."

Jase nodded, adjusting the collar on his casual flannel shirt. He poured coffee into a mug that read Have No Fear... The Attorney Is Here. "Last-minute Christmas shopping?" He handed the mug to Liam.

"I've got a flight leaving Aspen this afternoon."

He sensed the change in Jase, a stiffening of the other man's shoulders, as if he was already bracing himself for bad news. "Come on back, then." He led Liam into an office that looked like nothing had been put away for years. File cabinets lined the wall but stacks of cream-colored file folders sat in front of every one, some so high it would take only a wisp of a breeze to send them toppling.

"It's organized chaos," Jase said, taking a seat behind a large mahogany desk that was surprisingly tidy in comparison to the rest of the office.

"You lose your secretary?"

"I've lost three secretaries," Jase admitted with a sigh. "There's something in the water around here. Everyone I hire ends up pregnant." He laughed when Liam's brows rose. "Not by me."

"Another reason I'm holding on to Tanner. He's not going to get pregnant anytime soon."

Jase leaned back in his chair. "I'm guessing you didn't pull me out of bed before sunrise to critique my office decor."

Liam took a drink of coffee, his throat like sandpaper, then winced.

"Told you it was terrible," Jase muttered.

"LifeMap is going to Vermont."

"Feel free to beat around the bush next time." Jase put down his coffee, leaned forward as if he needed to catch his breath after being sucker punched.

"I'm sorry," Liam said, knowing how inadequate those two words sounded. "The official press release with the announcement will go out right after Christmas. I wanted you to hear it from me first."

"Is there anything I can do to change your mind?"

"No. Crimson isn't the right fit for the company. For me."

Jase glanced up. "Really? Because I didn't get that from you last night."

"Today isn't last night."

"Right. That statement might be deep and profound, but I'm too caffeine deprived to tell. If there's anything that will make a difference going forward, I'm still in the game. If not, best of luck in Vermont." He scrubbed his hands over his face, took a long swallow of coffee and cringed. "That's worse than usual. Seriously, let's head over to Life Is Sweet. The bear claws will be warm this early."

Liam's jaw dropped. "Are you for real? I just told you my million-dollar company has rejected Crimson. You're running for mayor next year."

"I was planning to run before you got to town, so you leaving won't derail me. Maybe this will hurt my chances, but that's my problem, not yours." Jase stood, gazed into his cup for a moment. "How can coffee be so difficult to get right?"

"You're missing the part where you yell at me, threaten to run me out of town for leading you on, tell me I've abused my wealth and power."

"Liam." Jase shook his head, walked around the desk.

"I think you just took care of that yourself. Am I upset that you're not headquartering here? Yes. Will life go on? Hell, yes. Crimson is a great town. Whether or not it's right for you doesn't change that."

"But why are you inviting me to the bakery?"

"Because…" Jase walked past Liam to the receptionist area, grabbing a performance jacket from a hook near the door. "I'm hungry and I need caffeine. We are not splitting the atom here, man."

Liam stood in the doorway between the two rooms as Jase turned. "Oh, wait. I get it. You think I won't want to hang out since you've kicked Crimson to the curb?"

"In a word…yes."

"I can't decide if you think so little of me or yourself." He opened the door to his office and sunlight streamed in as morning dawned. "I do know that Katie's going to be swamped in about fifteen minutes, and if I miss out on a bear claw because of your existential crisis, we *will* have words."

"Existential crisis," Liam repeated with a laugh, following Jase out the door. "Is that what this is?"

"Your business, not mine." Jase waved to a handful of people, volunteers it looked like to Liam, who'd begun sweeping and straightening around the square. "I'm a simple guy."

"Then I take it you don't have a girlfriend?"

"Nothing about women is simple."

"No doubt."

"How does Natalie feel about you leaving? It seemed like you two were getting close again."

"I'm not sure either of us really knows how to let someone get close."

"More deep thoughts." Jase rubbed his temple. "I need caffeine before I can go there." Just as they got to the bakery, he stopped and turned. "Natalie has had a hard time of it the past few years. It's not easy for her to trust people, to let anyone help. I think she is so used to taking care of things herself with the problems her mom's had."

"You know her pretty well."

Jase shrugged. "We grew up in the same area of town, and I was her attorney for the divorce."

Liam opened his mouth, but Jase held up a hand. "Attorney/client privilege prevents me from saying any more than that about Brad Holt or all the reasons he didn't deserve her. But I can tell you she's special, although you must know that already."

Liam looked away from Jase, down the street to the mountain that shadowed the town. One word was inadequate to describe all the things that made Natalie precious to him, made it so hard to walk away.

"She's a cactus," Jase continued, clearly warming to his topic. Sounding more as if he was giving a closing argument with every word. "A prickly pear on the surface, thorny and thick-skinned, but inside full of delicate sweetness."

Liam rolled his eyes, even as he had to admit the image fit. "Delicate sweetness? Who's getting existential now?"

A wide grin split Jase's face. "I know, man. Wait until I down that first cup of coffee. I'll get going for real then. Are you positive you have to leave town today? Christmas is right around the corner, and I'm sure it would mean a lot to Ruth to have you here."

A part of Liam wanted to stay, the young boy who had loved Christmas once upon a time. But the man he'd become knew he had to go, that if he stayed here longer it would only lead to more pain. He'd had quite enough hurt, both giving and receiving, to last a lifetime. Maybe he wanted to fool himself into thinking he'd changed, but he hadn't. He was the person he'd always been and what he did best was leave. Why wait?

"One more cup of coffee," he told Jase. "Then I'm out of here."

Natalie peeked around the corner of the bedroom and saw Ruth napping in her bed. Late afternoon light filtered through the sheer curtains at the window, bright despite the cold temperature outside. The older woman seemed peaceful but as she looked closer, she noticed dried tears tracked down her cheeks. Her throat tightened at the sight. It had only been two days since Liam had left Crimson. Natalie had kept herself extra busy during that time, which wasn't difficult right before Christmas. She and Ruth hadn't talked about Liam's departure, but she knew the older woman's heart was breaking as much as her own. It was simple to blame herself for their sadness.

She must have made a noise because Ruth stirred, her eyes opening. "Natalie," she whispered. "You're crying."

"No." Natalie wiped the back of her sleeve across her runny nose. "I don't cry, Ruth. I've told you that before."

"Come here." Ruth patted her hand on the quilt.

Natalie shook her head. "You can't want me here after what I did. I...made him go. This is all my fault." She realized her voice was shaking and she felt her knees start to give way.

"Please come here."

Natalie stumbled forward. Sobs wracking her body, she fell onto the bed next to Ruth, curled into the woman. Now that she'd unleashed the tears, they wouldn't stop. She cried for all the mistakes she'd made, all the things she'd tried to repair but couldn't because she was too broken herself to even know where to begin. They were big sloppy tears and there were so many—years' and years' worth.

Ruth rubbed a gentle hand against her back, shushed and soothed her.

"Why couldn't you ha-ave be-en my mom?" Natalie asked on a choked cry. "Maybe then I wouldn't have turned out so messed up."

"You're doing the best you can," Ruth murmured. "You always have. You're a good mother and a great nurse. You have friends who love you and an amazing son. From what I can see, you turned out just fine."

"But I don't have Liam." Natalie's voice broke as she spoke his name. "I pushed him away. I let him go." She tried to focus through her tears. "I ruined your Christmas, and he wanted to make this one the best ever."

"You didn't ruin anything. Yes, I'm sad that Liam's gone. But I believe he'll come back. This is his home. I know that in my heart, and I can only hope that his will lead him here again."

"He won't." Natalie hiccupped, took the tissue Ruth handed her. "I should have begged him to stay. I wanted to, but I'm too much of a coward. There is so much fear inside me, Ruth, I feel like it's eating away at me from the inside out. What if I turn into my mother?"

"Sweetie, that's not going to happen. You've hit some major speed bumps in life. But you'll get through it."

"Alone. Always alone. And someday Austin is going to grow up and leave, and I'll be alone again." She blew her nose into the tissue. "I'm sorry, that sounds ridiculous. I've been hiding so much for so long, it feels like I can't live any other way."

"Change is difficult for all of us," Ruth said gently, then took a deep breath. "I'm moving out of the farmhouse."

Natalie blinked, then sat up on the bed. "But you love it here. This is your home."

"It has been for many years," Ruth agreed. "But I can't ignore the fact any longer that it's too much for me to be out here on my own, even with your help. My mind and my body…they aren't what they used to be. Evergreen is a good facility. I have friends there. It's time for my next chapter."

"When?"

"After the holidays. One more Christmas here. You and Austin can stay as long as you like. It will be a lot of work to clean out this place before it's ready to go on the market. I'm not in any hurry to sell it." Her smile was wistful. "Baby steps."

Natalie thought about using those same words with Liam. "You are the bravest person I know." She leaned forward, kissed Ruth's wrinkled cheek. "I'm going to pay back the money you gave Brad," she said suddenly. She and Ruth hadn't talked any more about that revelation, but Natalie no longer wanted to avoid the hard truths of her life.

"I gave him that money freely," Ruth answered. "Although I see now that it was a mistake. Not to support you, but to encourage him in thinking there would be more. I thought he would leave you alone if I paid him enough."

"You'll never know how much it means to me that you did that, but Brad isn't your responsibility." She dabbed at her eyes with the corner of the tissue. "He isn't mine anymore, either. I talked to Jase and met with the sheriff about what's been going on. There's not much they can do about the money Brad already has, but I have backup now if he comes looking for more. I told Brad that I'm filing a petition for sole custody. There's nothing he can do to me anymore. Nothing I will let him do."

"How did he take this news?"

"He yelled and made threats, all of which Jase recorded. Then he cried and begged and when that didn't work, he told me exactly what he thought of Crimson and me. It wasn't pretty."

"I'm sorry, Natalie."

She shrugged, realizing that for all the poison her ex-husband had thrown at her, his words hadn't really touched her. "He'd invited my mom to the meeting for moral support, so the one positive was that she got to see his true nature. I don't know if that will change her feelings about him in the long run, but at least there's hope."

"There's always hope," Ruth agreed with a nod. She glanced at the clock on the nightstand. "I'm done napping. I need to get ready for the pageant tonight. How is Austin doing?"

"He is confused and sad that his dad won't be here for the pageant, but we're lucky to have so many people who love him. You top that list. You're family to him—to both of us."

"That goes both ways, sweetie, and I can't wait to see him perform."

Natalie climbed off the bed, held out a hand to Ruth to help her stand.

"I remember one year when Liam had the lead in the Christmas play at school." She tapped a finger on her chin. "He must have been around Austin's age, maybe third grade. He was Rudolph."

"He played a reindeer?" Natalie laughed at the thought.

"Complete with a red foam nose and papier-mâché antlers. He worked on those for hours and was so proud." Ruth suddenly looked sad. "His parents didn't show up that night. They missed the whole thing, sent their driver to record it so they could watch it later."

"How awful," Natalie murmured. Her heart broke at the thought of how Liam must have felt as a boy. "Liam must have been devastated."

Ruth nodded. "We watched him glancing out to the audience during the play, looking for them. He acted as if he didn't care, but it hurt him badly. After that he started getting into trouble. They couldn't ignore the regular summons to the principal's office. I think it was the only way he knew to get their attention."

Austin ran into the room at that moment. "Mom, I need to get to the school. I don't want to be late."

Natalie reached out and pulled her son into a tight hug. "We'll leave in a few minutes. I love you, buddy."

"You, too, Mom."

They got ready and drove to the school. The parking lot was almost full. It was a beautiful night, crisp and clear. Natalie dropped off Austin with his class, then walked with Ruth to the auditorium. There was so much excitement in the air, she could literally feel the love from the families, the holiday spirit. Again, her thoughts strayed to Liam, to a young boy looking for his parents and not finding them.

Her friends already had seats near the stage. Olivia and Logan sat with Millie and Jake and Jake's young daughter, Brooke.

"Is Austin going to sing loud?" Brooke asked as Natalie and Ruth joined them. "Can I clap for him?"

"Of course you can," Natalie answered, her heart swelling. This was what it meant to be loved, to grow up surrounded by people who helped you know you mattered. Everyone should know this feeling, and she realized she'd been keeping the people in her life at arm's length because of her own fear. She no longer wanted to be alone. She was ready to sail away from the emotional island she'd marooned herself on for so many years.

"Nat, it's about to start." Olivia tugged on her sleeve. "Are you going to sit down?"

She dropped into the chair next to her friend as the lights went down in the auditorium. "I have a favor to ask you," she whispered to Olivia. "Can you help me with something? I'll explain it after the pageant."

"Whatever you need," Olivia answered, taking her hand and giving it a squeeze.

The curtain opened, the elementary school band played and the kids started the first stanza of "I'll Be Home for Christmas." Austin met her gaze, gave a little wave as he sang. Natalie's heart sang along with him.

This, she thought, is going to be the best Christmas ever for all of them. She would make sure of that.

Chapter Eighteen

Liam buttoned up his overcoat as he walked out onto the sidewalk into the biting Chicago cold. A damp wind whipped off the lake, seeping into his bones and the gray sky made him miss the bright Colorado sun even more. Two weeks in the mountains and suddenly he felt like a stranger to the oppressive midwestern winter.

Not suddenly. He'd been a stranger in his own life for far too many years, but it was the connections—the friendships—he'd made in Colorado that forced him to realize it. That part of his life was over for good, and it wouldn't help him to dwell on it now.

Instead he took the few steps to the car waiting for him at the curb without looking around. Despite the cold, downtown was busy on Christmas Eve, with both last-minute shoppers and people coming to the city with family and friends to celebrate the holiday. Liam didn't need any more reminders that he'd be spending this Christmas alone.

He climbed into the back of the black sedan that Tanner had arranged to pick him up after his meeting with the LifeMap investors. But he wasn't alone in the backseat as the car pulled away from the curb.

"Merry Christmas, Liam."

"Dad." Liam pinched the bridge of his nose between two fingers. He knocked on the window between the front and back seats to get the driver's attention. "Can you turn off the music?" The car was silent a moment later.

"You have something against Bing Crosby?" his father asked.

"What do you want, Dad?" He kept his eyes trained to the window, watching the crowded sidewalks as the car made its way through the city. "I thought you'd be halfway to Fiji by this time."

"Bora Bora this year," his father clarified. "And I should be. We're flying out later this afternoon. Jena isn't happy, she had to reschedule our couple's massage."

Liam slanted his father a look at that statement. Michael held up his hands. "What can I tell you? It keeps her happy. Have you spoken to your mother?"

"No, and I don't expect to. Where is she this year? Ibiza?"

Michael made a dismissive grunt. "With that Eurotrash boyfriend of hers. She'll call at some point. The time change distracts her."

"You don't have to make excuses," Liam said between clenched teeth. "And I know you didn't hijack my car just to wish me a merry Christmas."

"I'd like to give you another chance to bring LifeMap to Donovan Enterprises. I want you to come back, Liam."

"Not going to—"

"Before you embarrass yourself."

"Excuse me?" Liam turned to look at his father, into

eyes so much like his own. His dad's gaze showed no emotion, never had.

"You can't think this venture is going to be a success."

"Actually, I do."

"Not if you handle everything on your own. You need the company's backing for something this big. The fact that you were actually entertaining Colorado as a viable option for the headquarters proves that. You've always had some kind of unhealthy attachment to Ruth Keller."

"Maybe because she cares about me."

His father waved away that argument like a pesky fly. "Don't forget she was my nanny, too. It was a mistake hiring her to help with you and letting you move out there in high school. You both seemed to forget she was an employee, not family. It's past time to cut the apron strings."

"The strings I'm cutting are with Donovan Enterprises. I left the company for good."

"The only reason investors are backing you is because of your association with Donovan."

"The company I headed for the last five years while you were busy with your couple's massages," Liam couldn't help but remind his father. He hated that his dad still had the power to pull him into these petty squabbles.

"You had a great team around you. A team I put there."

This was when Liam should begin to doubt himself and if he could ever live up to or live down his father's expectations. But he'd worked too hard to build LifeMap. He believed in the idea behind the brand and knew he was going to make it a success. "Would it be so beyond reason to think you'd be proud of me?"

Michael pointed a finger at Liam. "I knew it. This is just like when you were a kid, always having to rebel in some way. Is this some pathetic holdover cry for attention?"

Liam's mouth dropped open at the blatant cruelty of those words. He waited for the pain to slice through him, the sting of judgment and rejection. But nothing came. He felt nothing, which scared him almost as badly.

This wasn't the man he wanted to be, all investor lunches and new ventures. He knew that didn't bring happiness, his father was a living example of that. For a moment, he was tempted to simply walk away. Forget about LifeMap and move on to whatever was next. It would be easier than staying to fight, to face his father and his own fears.

He was sick of running. No matter how far and fast he went nothing he found ever filled the hollow place inside him. Nothing had until he'd returned to Crimson. To Natalie.

He tapped on the window again and signaled the driver to pull over. "I'm through, Dad. LifeMap is mine. My life is mine, what I make of it."

Michael grabbed his arm as Liam opened the door to the car. "Liam, wait. I'm sorry."

Liam didn't close the door again but looked over his shoulder at his father.

"I am proud of you and I want you back at Donovan Enterprises because you're good at what you do. The best, in fact. We need you and LifeMap. I need you."

While the words should have been a balm to his ego, he couldn't muster an emotional response. His father needed him because of what Liam could do for his company. The woman he'd left behind in Colorado needed him—wanted him—because of who he was on the inside. She wanted his heart, and as scared as it made him, Liam was finally ready to give it to her. He only hoped it wasn't too late.

"I'm not coming back." He shook off his father's grasp.

"I'm moving forward with my life, and you aren't a part of it." He stepped out of the car, then ducked his head back in. "Enjoy that couple's massage," he said and slammed shut the door.

He walked the few blocks to his apartment building on his cell phone, no longer feeling the cold. There were too many plans to make, plans that warmed him from the inside out.

Dashing into the lobby, he waved to the doorman.

"Mr. Donovan there's a—"

"No time," Liam called over his shoulder, ducking into the elevator before the doors closed. "Merry Christmas."

His toe tapped impatiently on the marble as the elevator rose to the top floor. He glanced at his watch and typed a quick text to Tanner. He had less than an hour to get packed and to the airport. He wasn't going to miss this chance.

He started toward his bedroom, then stopped and sniffed the air. Lavender. The air was scented with the delicate fragrance that had haunted his dreams for the past several nights. Pivoting on his heel, he turned toward the wall of windows that overlooked Lake Michigan from his living room.

His heart thundered in his chest at the sight before him. Natalie lay asleep on his couch, her blue parka bright against the sofa's deep leather.

Natalie jerked awake from a dream, the same one she'd been having since Liam left Crimson. She was searching for him, running through the woods, calling his name. But every time she got close a wall would appear in front of her, so tall and wide she couldn't see around or over, couldn't figure out a way to pass. That was usually when she woke up, shaking and shivering and alone in bed. But today there was a rumbling in her dream and as if it had been struck by lightning, the wall crumbled. Through the dust and debris she saw Liam standing on the other side. As she moved toward him, her eyes popped open.

For a moment she closed them again, wanting to return to the dream, to discover how this new twist might change the ending. Then she blinked, glanced around and remembered where she was.

Liam, flesh and blood Liam, who was so much better than dream Liam, stood right in front of her.

"Hey," she whispered.

He continued to stare.

"I hope you're not mad. Tanner called the doorman to let me in. I flew in on the red-eye this morning, but you were in a meeting so I thought I'd wait here."

Still no response.

Not exactly how she'd planned this to go.

"If you're busy," she mumbled, feeling like the fool she was, "I can leave."

"I have a plane to catch. Chartered."

"Oh." The one word came out on a puff of air, all that was left in her lungs. Her throat closed up, and she couldn't breathe. Wondered if she'd ever take a full breath again. Somehow she managed to scramble to her feet, her eyes on the ground.

Before she could take a step, Liam had moved forward, crowding her. Smelling like the cold and the city and himself. Stupidly, she wanted to press her nose to his throat.

"You flew to Chicago," he whispered. "You got on an airplane on Christmas Eve."

Tucking her hair behind her ears, she tried to smile. Tried to make her voice light. "It's a surprisingly good time to fly. The airport was empty at midnight." She zipped up her coat with shaking fingers. "I needed the practice, anyway, if I'm going to take Austin to the beach for spring break. Takeoff and landing were the worst." She forced a laugh. "I'm pretty sure I only screamed once. Or twice. Well, merry Christmas, then. I'll get out of your way."

"Natalie." His finger touched her chin, tipped it up even as she resisted.

"Don't worry about it, Liam. I knew it was a long shot, but—"

"I'm flying to Colorado. Back to you." He wiped away the tear that fell from the corner of her eye. "I thought you had a rule about crying."

"That was a stupid rule," she said with a sniff. "And in the past week I've just about caught up for all those years of not crying. Turns out a lot of things in my life didn't make sense." She bit down on her lip. "At least without you they didn't."

"I love you, Natalie."

She drew in a deep, shuddering breath, her lungs returning to life with a vengeance. "If I'm going to be a crier, I need to learn to cry pretty. Enough with the ugly tears."

"Sweetheart, you are beautiful to me no matter what." He wrapped his arms around her, pulled her against him, his own breath uneven.

She held on tight, promising herself she would never let go of this man. "I love you right back, Liam Donovan. So much. I'm sorry I didn't tell you before, didn't beg you to stay."

"I should have never left," he whispered against her neck, trailing soft kissing up and along her jaw. "I will never leave you again, Natalie. No more running. Anything that happens, we face it together. I should have been the man you could trust with anything. I'll work the rest of my life to be that for you."

"Come home, Liam." She drew back, took his face in her hands. "You don't belong in Chicago or Vermont. Crimson is your home."

"You are my home, Nat." The emotion in his eyes melted her. "Wherever you are is where I need to be."

She pressed her mouth to his, knowing she would love this man for the rest of her life—and finally understanding that home wasn't a cage, it was the place that set you free.

Epilogue

Three Months Later

Natalie's head broke through the water to the sound of Austin whooping with delight.

"How do you do such a good handstand in the water, Mom? Your legs are totally straight." He bobbed up and down in the deep green ocean water of the Caribbean.

She laughed as she slicked the hair back from her face. "I convinced your grandma to let me take gymnastics when I was a kid. It was my favorite thing."

A group of kids called to Austin from a short way down the beach. He glanced at Natalie. "Those are the boys I met yesterday. They're on spring break from Indiana. Can I go help them with the sand castle?"

"Of course. I'll be here if you need anything."

Austin swam toward the beach and then, as the water got shallow, ran toward his new friends. Natalie followed him out of the water more slowly, adjusting her new bathing suit as she went. It was modest for a bikini, but showed a lot more skin than her old suit. But any feelings of self-consciousness she had disappeared as her gaze caught on Liam watching her from the lounge chair near the water's edge. He'd lifted his aviator sunglasses to the top of his head, his eyes held an intense mix of love and desire.

"Did I hear you say you were a gymnast?" He stood as she got closer, and her body gave its usual tingly reaction to him. His board shorts rode low on his hips and, after four days at the beach, his skin was golden. It gave her an extra thrill to know all that perfection was hers.

He wrapped a thick white towel around her, bending to nip her shoulder as he did.

"Two years at the old community center in Crimson," she said with a smile. "Want me to show you more of my moves?"

He whirled her around so quickly she squeaked. The kiss he gave her was gentle since they weren't alone on the beach, but it held the promise of so much more. "I want to see all your moves, Nat."

"Thank you for taking us on this vacation," she whispered against his mouth. "Saint Thomas is more beautiful than I could have imagined." She glanced toward her son, bent over the sand castle with his new friends. It was perfect on the island, the sun shining and blue skies overhead. A warm breeze blew off the ocean waves. It was hard not to feel content in a place like this. "I don't think Austin will ever want to leave."

"It's been fun." With one finger, he traced a droplet of water down the side of her face. "You've been fun."

Her smile widened. "I'm fun," she murmured. "Who knew?"

"I did."

Natalie kissed him again, then sank onto the lounge chair, positioning herself so she could keep an eye on Austin. She held Liam's hand, tugging him down to sit next to her. It was companionable, holding hands with him, their toes together in the sand. She continued to feel that storm of attraction for him, but it was these little moments that meant the most to her. She glanced at the ring on her finger, the perfect round diamond sparkling in the sunlight. Liam had proposed on New Year's Eve, telling her that this year was a new start for both of them. Joy was like a companion now, always with her when she'd felt alone for so long.

"What are you thinking about?" Liam asked.

She rested her head on his shoulder. "How happy I am. I never imagined…"

She swallowed as her voice caught on the swirl of emotions inside her. She swiped her fingers under her eyes. "Good tears," she said when Liam pulled her closer. "I cry at everything now. Commercials, songs on the radio. It's embarrassing."

"It's sweet," he countered.

"I never imagined," she began again, clearing her throat, "this kind of happiness was possible for me."

"Love will do that for you."

"You do that for me." It was true. Since Liam had returned with her to Crimson, Natalie had found the strength she needed to make real changes in her life. She would have managed it somehow on her own, but it was so much better with Liam's love and support. There were still hurdles. She had a date in three weeks for the final custody hearing, and although Brad wasn't fighting her anymore she'd feel better when her petition for sole custody was approved. Her relationship with her mother was still strained, and Trudy hadn't accepted Liam yet, but they'd all met for coffee last week at the bakery and it had been almost civil. *Baby steps*, she reminded herself.

"How are you feeling about the meeting with your dad?" They were flying through Atlanta tomorrow on the way back to Colorado, with an extended layover to have dinner with Natalie's father.

She met Liam's gentle gaze, no longer needing to hide her feelings. "Nervous but hopeful. The emails we've sent and the phone calls have been good. I'm grateful for the chance to get to know him finally." It had been difficult for her to get the nerve to contact the man after so many years of feeling rejected, but her father had been both apologetic and anxious to know her more. "I'm glad it wasn't too late."

"It's never too late to have the life you want, to be the person you're supposed to be" Liam whispered, pressing a kiss to her temple. "You taught me that, Nat. I love you for that and so many other reasons."

She sighed. "I love you, too, Liam." Her voice broke and she waved her fingers in front of her face. "Oh, no, here come the tears again."

"Tears of joy or sorrow," he told her. "I'll take them all as long as they're yours. As long as you are mine."

"I'm yours forever, Liam. Forever and always."

* * * * *

  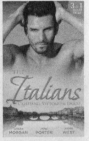

MILLS & BOON®

The Rising Stars Collection!

1 BOOK FREE!

This fabulous four-book collection features 3-in-1 stories from some of our talented writers who are the stars of the future! Feel the temperature rise this summer with our ultra-sexy and powerful heroes. Don't miss this great offer—buy the collection today to get one book free!

Order yours at
www.millsandboon.co.uk/risingstars

MILLS & BOON®

Cherish™

EXPERIENCE THE ULTIMATE RUSH OF FALLING IN LOVE